THE NEW LAW IN TOWN

"I see that judge made you a sheriff," Powers said. "That don't mean a goddamn thing to me. I'd as soon use that star as a target as not. I'm gonna tell you…"

"What you're going to do is listen, Powers," I snarled. "Don and me are going to clean up Gila Bend. There's no more free rides for you and your crew, no collections from the saloon owners, no gunfights in the street, no horse racing in the street. I hear your gamblers are crooked. Get rid of them. I hear you mistreat the whores and don't pay them 'cept with nickels and dimes. That'll stop. Lemme make this clear: starting right now, you people pay for what you drink or take out of the mercantile, you cut out the gunfights, and you pay your girls what they're worth. Anything else I think of, I'll let you know about."

Powers shook his head in amazement. "You're purely crazy," he said. "An' you won' 'ave Gila Bend alive. That's a promise!"

Outlaw Lawman

Paul Bagdon

LEISURE BOOKS   NEW YORK CITY

This one is for Bonnie Frankenberger—a sweet lady, a fine writer, and a wonderful and true friend.

A LEISURE BOOK®

June 2009

Published by

Dorchester Publishing Co., Inc.
200 Madison Avenue
New York, NY 10016

ISBN 10: 0-8439-6015-9
ISBN 13: 978 0 8439 6015 0
E-ISBN: 978-1-4285-0683-1

The name "Leisure Books" and the stylized "L" with design are trademarks of Dorchester Publishing Co., Inc.

Printed in the United States of America.

10 9 8 7 6 5 4 3 2

Visit us on the web at www.dorchesterpub.com.

Outlaw
Lawman

Chapter One

I heard the baseball game before I even drew close to it: men whooping and yelling, guns firing, the occasional series of curse words that reached me even over the distance. A sign on a stout fence post told me I was in—or coming into—Gila Bend.

I topped an easy rise and looked directly down at the game. A fat man was at bat. The pitcher gave him a good throw, and the fat man swung hard and arced the ball over the pitcher's head and into the outfield. It looked like an easy single, even though the heavy man waddled rather than ran. When he reached first base, the baseman swung at him, connected with his chin, and dropped him there in the dust, unconscious. A mixture of cheers and boos sounded as the fat man's pals dragged him off to the side.

The runner who'd been on second base took off for third as soon as the fat man connected with the ball. The third baseman covered his base—blocked it, actually—and held a thick piece of a tree branch. The runner dove at the baseman, and

1

the two of them rolled about in the dirt, raising a cloud of dust, punching, gouging, biting, and cursing. The runner managed to wrestle the club away from the baseman and beat him unconscious with it. At the same time, the runner who'd been on third was digging for home plate, running hard, knees pumping, head down, arms flailing. It was then that a loop sailed out from the group of observers. Whoever he was, he was one hell of a roper. His loop was small—exactly the right size to drop over the runner's head and stop him very quickly—so quickly, in fact, that the wet snap of his neck was easily audible over the rest of the racket of the game.

If the baseball game was a fuse, the fight that followed was the explosion. Two masses of bellowing, drunken men met about midfield, swinging, kicking, and in some cases, shooting.

I'd seen lots of bar fights, more than a few gunfights where the loser ended up dead, but I'd never seen anything like this before. Baseball can raise a man's ire, and a little pushing and maybe slugging is to be expected during a game, particularly when most or all of the players were drunk.

But damn: shooting a base runner? Snapping a fellow's neck with a lariat? Anybody who threw a loop the way that cowboy had could have widened it a foot or so and made his catch around the runner's middle.

My horse was getting antsy under me, catching the scent of the horses staked and hobbled down by the game. A slug whispered by my head, then another. A man never forgets that sound once he's heard it, and I've heard it too many times to sit around and wait to hear it again. I heeled my good bay horse into a gallop, swinging back down below the rise, and made a big half circle around the baseball game. From there it was easy enough to follow wagon tracks and hoofprints to Gila Bend.

I swung off the tracks and rode a half mile or so out onto the prairie. The money in my saddlebags was in those waterproof canvas sacks banks and large mercantiles use. I triangulated a nice little rock outcropping with a pair of desert pines, moved some rocks around, and stashed my money. Then I went on back to the trail that led to Gila Bend.

The town looked like most of the little Texas towns of the time—splintered, unpainted wood buildings; hand-painted signs; and the usual array of businesses: a stable, a mercantile, five saloons, a restaurant, a furniture maker/embalmer/mortician, and what may or may not have been at one time a church. It'd been burned, but it looked as though some of the chairs inside may once have been pews.

There were two or three horses tied in front of each gin mill and a few men walking, going into the mercantile or a saloon. Every man I saw was carrying a sidearm, and some carried two.

Some of the men were wearing those big broad hats—sombreros—and I knew for an absolute fact that any cowhand, drifter, saddle-tramp gambler—any American at all—would prefer to have his head broiled over a campfire like chicken than wear one of those Mex hats.

Without being obvious about it, I looked more closely at some of the men under sombreros. I was certain that looking too long at any man in Gila Bend was a bad idea. There was no doubt the fellows were Mexicans.

I was real unclear as to where I was, Texas or Mexico. I figured that in a hellhole like Gila Bend, it didn't much matter.

I put my horse up at the stable, had new shoes put on him all the way 'round, and paid in advance for a double scoop of crimped oats daily, plus all the good hay he wanted. That horse had done some hard and long traveling, and he more than deserved a respite, some good grub, and some time out from under the saddle.

I walked down the rutted street past the first saloon I came to. The beer and booze were singing out to me, but I kept walking. I was looking for a specific and recognizable man, and I knew I'd eventually find him.

I walked by what had once been a sheriff's office. The front door was battered and broken and hung from its top hinge. It was riddled with bullet holes, too. I looked inside as I walked by. There was an overturned rolltop desk that was partially burned. A cut chain hung from what had obviously been a rifle cabinet. There was a Stetson on the floor near the desk with several bullet holes in it and flaking, dried blood around the holes. It'd probably been a fine hat at one time; Stetson didn't make junk.

There's always at least one of the bar-rags I was looking for in Texas towns; I figured Gila Bend would have a couple of them—Mexican or Texan—and perhaps three. They were hard-core drunks, who, since they were incapable of working and too stupid to steal, spent their days cadging or begging drinks. Sometimes they exchanged good information for a belt of redeye and a schooner of beer. Often the information was mindless babble or pure fabrication; once in a while it was good.

I almost passed a barbershop, but then took a couple of steps back and entered. A bath was thirty cents, which was kind of steep. The shave and the haircut came to two bits.

The barber was a surly oaf who smelled of pomade, talcum powder, and stale beer. Usually those fellows would talk your ear off about nothing, but this guy was an exception. He grunted every so often as he went about his work but said not a word. When we evened up, I added a nickel tip, which was customary.

The barber's eyes opened wide in a parody of joyous surprise. "Hot goddamn!" he said. "Now I can buy me a few hundred acres of good land and a thousand head of prime, fat beef, an' maybe even a runnin' horse, an' make yet more money!"

I took the nickel back from the counter and put it in my pocket. "Hey, Mister . . ." he began angrily.

"Another word and I'll step on your goddamn

face real hard, you pile of shit," I said. The barber snorted and glared but didn't say anything.

I stood there a moment, trying to convince myself that doing what I had in mind made no sense at all. I couldn't do it. There was a shelf behind the barber chair that held maybe ten or so bottles of various stuff—cologne and such. I drew and blew the living piss out of six of them. The barber had hit the floor and was curled into a ball like a dung beetle. I stood there while I reloaded and then went on my way.

There was a burned-out building next to the barbershop and the next business was a saloon with a broad, poorly lettered sign over its batwings that said BAR—DRINK. Just outside was where the bar-rag latched on to me.

"Ahh, my good friend," he slurred as he stepped in front of me from where he'd been standing just outside the saloon. The man was a textbook illustration of what constant drunkenness, dissolution, malnutrition, and general booze-generated stupidity could do to a fellow. The poor sonofabitch wasn't worth the bullet it'd take to put him out of his misery.

"You looking for a drink?" I asked.

"I don't generally imbibe spirits, but I see that you're new in Gila Bend, and I'll be pleased to join you—on you, of course."

I was more than a tad astonished at how well this rummy spoke. I pushed through the batwings and held one side open for the man. As he passed me, I got a closer look at him. His hair was gray—

he wore no hat—and it seemed to have fallen out in lumps, leaving deathly pallid patches of scalp behind. It seemed to me that he was too gaunt to live; his wrists were like sticks, and his neck was so thin that his Adam's apple appeared to be the size of a ripe melon. He wore a work shirt that at one time must have belonged to a shorter man— the cuffs barely passed his elbows. His coveralls— large enough to accommodate three men his size—hung from his shoulders like drapes. His feet were bare and horrible to look upon; the nails of his toes were long and a vomit yellow hue, and the grime on his ankles and the upper length of his foot would be impossible to remove. It was part of his flesh, part of his being. The stench of his body was bad; I gagged as he walked past me. He smelled dead—long dead.

I picked up two schooners of beer, two shot glasses, and a bottle of Kentucky bourbon and carried all that on a tray to where my new colleague was sitting at a table. "My name's Pound," I said. "Yours?"

"I'm called Calvin," he said, "although various bartenders and others have different names for me—bad names, names that sometimes hurt."

I couldn't help asking, "Then why not crawl out of the bottle and do something with yourself?"

Calvin poured a shot with a trembling hand, spilling as much booze on the table as he got into the shot glass. He drained his schooner in one long, gulping, gasping swallow. He followed the beer immediately with the shot. " 'Cause I don't want to," he said. "Bein' a bar-rag suits me. It ain't the noblest of professions, but it works for me." He refilled his shot glass with considerable less shaking this time and dumped it down, smacking his lips as if he'd just had a bite of a crisp, tart apple. "I suspect you're looking for information—or did you set up drinks to ask me the name of my tailor?"

I poured myself a shot. "Tell me about Gila Bend," I said.

"It got started maybe twenty years ago when a fat vein of silver was struck. The vein didn't play out, neither. It's a little harder to get to these days, but she's still there. 'Course that strike brought lots of others: miners, gamblers, men running from the law, drifters still wearing Reb uniforms, whores, gunfighters, storekeepers, saloons, an' so forth, just like any burg built on gold or silver does."

"Why'd they name it Gila Bend?"

"'Cause there was a Gila setting right where a miner hit the strike."

"Let me ask you this: are we in Texas or Mexico?"

"Calvin laughed. "Texas—not that it matters much. You could throw a stone from here to Mexico."

"What about the law here?"

Calvin grimaced and spat on the floor. "Shit," he said, "you might have seen the sheriff's office. He was the fourth one in less than three years. Got shot off his horse from a hundred or better yards away by a fella with a Sharps. The one before him was a little slower on the draw than a shootist who'd moved in. The one before that . . . well, I think he got a knife in his heart trying to break up a fracas in a saloon. I disremember what happened to the one farthest back, but you can wager he didn't die from falling out of bed and cracking his head."

I handed Calvin a pair of ten-cent pieces and had him fetch a couple more beers for us. When he sat down at the table again, Calvin said, "There's a fellow by the name of Billy Powers. Billy runs Gila Bend."

"How so?"

"It just happened, I guess. There's paper out on him and most of his men. They rode in and decided to stay. None of them have much use for Mexico or Mexicans, so they didn't care to cross over. There's a bunch of Mexicans in Gila Bend, but they walk real quiet around Billy Powers."

"What's the paper on Powers for?" I asked.

"Murder and rape, robbery, the usual stuff. He's a hired-gun type. He'd shoot his grandmother if the money was adequate."

"Sounds like a swell guy."

Calvin laughed, but it was a bad laugh, one with no mirth behind it.

"There's paper out on maybe half the men in town, Pound. And the other half just haven't killed or robbed enough to rate posters."

"How'd this Powers come to take over the town?"

"Well," Calvin said, "four—maybe five—years ago, Billy beat the piss out of a man who was feared by everyone in Gila Bend. This was a fistfight in a saloon, and it didn't take but a minute or so."

I nodded.

"The very next day, Billy was in a saloon where he fancied a whore. He wrestled her clothes off—everything she was wearing—in front of a packed saloon, mind you. Then he slapped her on the ass and carried her upstairs. In a minute she was screaming in pain. Somebody ran for the sheriff, and one of his men warned Billy. They met on the street in front of the saloon. Billy put three slugs in the sheriff's chest before the lawman's pistol ever cleared leather."

I rolled a smoke and pushed my sack of tobacco and my papers across the table to Calvin. He rolled a cigarette that looked every bit as good as one of those fancy-ass store-boughts. He looked longingly at the sheath of papers and the sack of tobacco in front of him as I struck a lucifer and lit both our smokes.

"Keep 'em," I said. "I got plenty more."

His full smile showed how very few teeth he had, and the ones left were more brown than yellow, slanted like very old headstones in an ancient cemetery. His gums were a godawful greenish-pink that made my gorge rise hot and stinging in the back of my throat. I had to look away.

I took a long suck of beer. "Why doesn't the law come in and tear this whole goddamned place down?" I asked.

" 'Cause it ain't worth the time nor the soldiers who'd be killed—and there'd be a whole lot of them."

I needed to think for a time, and then I said, "You're either diddling me or running some sort of a scam. I don't like either choice."

"I don't know what you're . . ."

"Talking about," I finished Calvin's sentence. "It's this: your language. Your use of words swings from that of a drunken cowhand to that of a college professor and back, often in the same sentence. What's going on here?"

Calvin poured us each another shot of whiskey. "I was once an instructor in a school in Massachusetts," he said. "It was a good job, but I drank my way out of it. Then I came West and taught at a school in a town called Hempton's Stop, and boozed my way out of that one, too. Somehow I ended up here after a couple of years." He looked at me quizzically. "What was it that indicated to you that I—"

I interrupted again. "*Indicated?* How many cowhands or hard-core drunks would use that word?"

"I guess maybe you're a college man, too," he said.

"I was. I was a drunk, too, almost as bad as you. Hell, I'd drink stale beer out of a hog's ass."

"But you beat it."

"Hell, no. I still want more all the time. But a few years back I partnered up with a good man and we robbed banks and I got the booze under control."

Paul Bagdon

Calvin stared at the wall behind me. After a moment, he said, "When I was a kid I had this friend named Abimilech."

"Abimilech?"

"It's a biblical name. Anyway, Abe's father made 'shine. We were maybe twelve years old when we took a few belts and got silly and clumsy. But the difference was that Abe had had enough, puked, and passed out. I wanted more—a whole lot more. And . . . well . . . I was off and running from that day forward."

We were silent for a long moment. Finally, Calvin said, "I guess you'll be riding out later today."

"No. I figured I'd spend a couple days here, rest up my horse."

"Well," Calvin grinned, "this is one place the law won't catch up with you."

For some reason that peeved me a bit. "What makes you think I'm running from the law—or from anyone else?"

"No offense, Pound. But Gila Bend isn't what you'd call a quiet town to relax in."

"I've been in a slew of places as bad or worse than this dung heap," I said. "Either a fast gun and his boys kill the lawman and take over a town, or they string up a couple of the townsfolk to keep the others in line. And I'm still sitting here, aren't I?"

"Sure," Calvin said. After a moment he added, "Feisty, ain't you?"

"I'm just passing through," I repeated. I pushed back my chair and stood.

12

Calvin cackled. "Passing through? To where? Hell? No need to leave, Pound. C'mon, sit down." His hand was wrapped protectively around the whiskey bottle, as if I were about to snatch it from him. I thought it over for a moment and then sat down.

"This Powers," I said. "How many men does he have here?"

"Maybe thirty to forty. The number kind of varies actually. Some can't take Powers's craziness and ride out at night—and keep ridin', I guess 'til they run their horse's legs down to nubs. Then there's Powers's shoot-outs, too. That drops a few men each year."

"Shooting contests?"

Calvin grimaced. "Powers chooses a couple of men at random and puts them out in the street facing one another at about twenty-five to thirty paces. The men draw—they know they have no option, no way out. Powers stands there with a .30-30 just to make sure no one hightails it." Calvin cleared his throat. "The one who's alive at the end wins."

"Powers has no argument with these two men?"

"Nope. He'll get liquored up an' something will piss him off and he grabs a couple of fellows and drags them outside. No reason at all for it, Pound. Lots of times the guys are friends. That's sad."

"Couldn't the ones in the street both turn on Powers and blow his ass off?"

"That's been tried. The rest of the group blew the two men to pieces. That's one of the rules."

The complete and utter depravity of a man who'd demand a gunfight to the death between two others who more than likely had nothing at all against each other stunned me. Even Bloody Bill and his lunatics didn't quite reach Billy Powers's depth of killing simply for the sake of killing. I looked at the bottle in front of Calvin. It was about two-thirds gone. I filled my shot glass. "If I got jammed up in a situation like that, I'd take out the man I was drawing against and then empty my pistol into Powers. If his boys shot me to pieces after that, I'd die with a smile on my face."

Calvin nodded. "That makes good sense. I've often wondered if Powers's gang saw him dead and bleeding in the street, whether they'd scatter like a bunch of puppies in a thunderstorm. Powers is what holds them together, and without him they'd be nothing—and they know that."

"They're nothing already," I said.

"Yeah, but they have a leader."

"Right, a leader who's a homicidal maniac." I stood again. "Thanks for the information, Calvin," I said. "It was appreciated. You keep that bottle." I reached into my vest and pulled out a ten-dollar bill. "I don't want to insult you, but maybe you could use a . . . loan . . . of ten dollars?"

Calvin laughed his annoying cackle. "Insult me? Hell, you can insult me all day long with them tens, Pound." He held out a grimy hand with enough crud under his fingernails to give a maggot the heaves. I'm a little ashamed of this—dirty or not, the guy was still a man—but I looked as if I was fussing in my vest with my right hand and turned away, heading toward the batwings, as if I considered our meeting and conversation over. I heard the grating cackle behind me.

I took a deep breath as soon as I stepped outside. The reek of tobacco smoke, spilled beer, sweat, and the essence of a gathering of long-unwashed men was pervasive, and it followed me like a foul and disgusting cloud until I was several steps away from the saloon. I glanced back and found that the cloud I imagined was real; smoke and stink billowed out the batwings.

It was coming dusk, and the softening light made Gila Bend appear almost pretty, like a rendering of a quiet Texas town by an Easterner. The pianos in the saloons began to tinkle almost melodically. A pair of men—hardcases from the looks of them—rode down the street toward me. I noticed that both of their horses were gaunt and hadn't been groomed in a long time. As the men drew closer, I could see scabbed-over spur marks on the flanks of the animals.

The two men could just as well have been cut with the same mold. They slouched in their saddles, looking almost asleep, but their eyes missed nothing. One wore a pair of Colts in holsters on his hips, the other a single pistol on a hip but another strapped over his shoulder and across his chest. Both riders could have benefited by being dragged through a sheep-dip. Each had perhaps a week's growth of beard and greasy hair that hung past his shoulders in thick hanks.

They moved away to the side of each other as they approached me, which I didn't like much. Close together, both could have been taken down by a good shootist, but spread apart, the man in the middle would die. Unconsciously, I pushed my coat back behind the butt of my Colt and let my hand linger there. The one on my right lifted the barrel of the .30-30 in his saddle scabbard a couple of inches, not pointing directly at me, but not far off, either.

We stood there for a full minute without moving, as if we were statues. Finally, I said, "Evening, gents. That cool breeze feels real good, doesn't it?"

The one who answered—the man on the left—said, "Maybe it does, maybe it don't," in such a high-pitched, childish voice I had to bite the inside of my mouth to keep from laughing. My eyes dropped for a moment to his throat. An elevated, festering scar ran from one ear, under his chin, and almost to the other ear.

"Shaddup, Squeaky," the Right Man said. To me, he said, "New in our little town?" in a voice that was near worn out from tobacco and whiskey.

"Just kind of passing through—resting my horse a bit, have a drink or two, maybe play a little poker."

"You looking for work?" Right asked.

"Nope. Just drifting."

"What do you do when you are working?" Right asked.

"This an' that," I said. "I work beef some— whatever comes along when I'm in need of money."

"Bullshit," Squeaky snapped. "You got no rope on your saddle and your hands look like them of one of them pansy-boys."

I laughed. "And you sure do sound like one."

Squeaky went for his pistol. I blew him off his horse before he had a chance to bring his barrel at me. I swung immediately to Right, ready to fire, but he was just sitting there in his saddle rolling a cigarette.

"That goddamn voice can sure get on a man's nerves after a bit," he said. "Like a goddamn ol' rusty gate cryin' out for oil every time it's opened."

"Your friend a mite touchy about it?"

"Shit, Squeaky's touchy about everything." He grinned. "Or he was until you plugged him, any-ways."

"Maybe a fellow like that," I said, "ought to keep his yap shut 'til he gets a whole lot handier with his weapon."

"Could be," Right said noncommittally. "Say, you fancy a drink?"

"Another time," I said. "I'm just takin' a little walk, like I said."

Right's voice became flinty and cold. "I'd sug-gest you have that drink with me—let me tell you about Gila Bend."

Paul Bagdon

I waited a few seconds but not too many. "Sure," I said, "let's do that."

"My name's Mack."

"Mine's Pound."

There was no offer to shake hands on either part.

Mack walked his horse over to the rail of the saloon I'd just left, swung down, and tied up.

"What about that?" I asked, nodding toward the corpse still leaking blood into the dust and grit of the street.

"Ain't nothin'. It'll get took care of."

We went into the saloon. Mack walked over to a table where four men were playing cards. There wasn't a word exchanged, but each picked up his money and cards and found another table.

"You the lawman here?" I asked.

Mack chuckled. "In a sense, maybe. I ride with Billy Powers, an' anyone who rides with him is a kind of a lawman—we make our own laws." He found his own attempt at humor hilarious and laughed like the braying of a mule.

I forced a grin. "Who's this Billy Powers?"

A bartender brought a bottle and two glasses and hurried off. "Billy," Mack said, "owns Gila Bend—every whore, every bottle, the mercantile, the other store, the livery, the assay office—the whole shebang. He moved in with a few men—afore my time—and just took over. An' here we are—four dead lawmen later."

I nodded as if impressed. "He must have come

in with a basketful of money to buy up all the businesses," I said.

Mack brayed again. "Buy? Buy, my ass! He jus' took 'em over, an' a percentage of the take of each place goes right into his pocket."

"Sounds like a sweet deal to me, Mack," I said. I poured each shot glass full. We both downed the whiskey. My surprise must have shown on my face: the booze was smooth and smoky. "The swill," Mack explained, "goes to the town people. The good stuff is reserved for Billy an' his men."

"I don't get it," I said. "The people let Billy Preston just—"

"Powers."

"Sorry, Powers. Anyway they let Billy and his men jus' ride in an' take over?"

"Some didn't. You can see them from the little rise outside town. Boot Hill, it's called."

"Well, that's one way to keep peace in a town," I said.

"Lemme ask you this," Mack said. "You wanted? Is there money on your head?"

"Maybe," I said.

I felt something hard pressing against my right kneecap.

Mack grinned wolfishly. "Ever see what a .45 will do to a kneecap? It ain't real pretty. Either the fella bleeds out and croaks, or a doc saws the sumbitch off a couple inches above the wound, 'cause of gangrene." He paused for a moment. "So let's cut out this 'maybe' horseshit."

I remained silent a few moments longer. That goddamn .45 felt as big as the maw of a canon against my knee. Mack was right about bullet-shattered kneecaps. Hell, I'd rather take a slug between the eyes.

"You got eight hundred dollars in your saddle-bag, Pound. That ain't the kinda money a man draws for following a herd—'specially without a throwin' rope an' a bedroll no cowpuncher would tie onto his saddle. So where'd the money come from, Pound?"

I grinned at Mack. "No matter how many of my knees you shoot up, I'm still faster than you and better than you."

"Bullshit. But you an' me might just find that out someday, no?"

"Oh, yeah," I said. "You can bet on that."

"Seems to me you already are bettin', Pound. Now, what about the money?"

"My poke came from a pimp outside of Yuma. I had a bit of a fancy for one of his whores. She was a pretty girl—not like the goddamn buffalo cows you have here. One day I saw some bad bruises on her ass and back. Her pimp—name of Spenser—found out she was pleasuring me most afternoons and he wasn't getting his cut. This Spenser had a bodyguard outside his room. At that time I figured I was a tough young buck, and I was carrying a pair of .45s. I emptied one into the guard and the other into the pimp. I found his poke under his bed—damned near four thousand dollars. Then I hauled ass. So, about paper on me,

I don't know. I just wandered and drifted, spending the pimp's money."

I didn't have to make up the story as I went along; it was true.

"Where's the rest of the cash?"

"Like I said, I pissed it away—I've got maybe six hundred in my pocket plus the eight you found—and that's the end of it. Tell you the truth, I came through here to see if you folks had a bank I could do some work in. If not, the assay office would work out, too."

"Woulda been one big goddamn mistake," Mack said.

"I can see that now."

The muzzle of the pistol slipped away from my knee, and I could hear the oiled *shuff* as he holstered the gun. That made my breathing a lot easier and more even.

Mack poured more whiskey for both of us. "I seen you get your coat out of the way of your Colt, Pound. You one of these crazy-fast gunmen like Doc Holliday or maybe Wyatt himself?"

Maybe it was the whiskey talking for me: I should have shut up. "Holliday uses a goddamn shotgun he carries under his duster. He's got consumption or something, and he coughs most of the time when he isn't sucking air. I imagine I could blow him straight to hell before he fumbled out the scatter gun. Holliday is one of those fellows—like Billy the Kid—who lives on luck and backshooting and reputation."

"What about Earp?"

"Different story. I never met the man. I never saw him in trouble, in a gunfight. I hear he's real fast and shoots well, and I heard that from men I trust, men I could believe. Maybe I could drop him; maybe I couldn't. I don't know—or care."

Mack chuckled. "Ain't you somethin'? You figure there's anyone in this place who could take you? Some of the gamblers are good, and there are a few of Billy Powers's men here."

"No," I said. "Not face to face anyway. Any one of them could take me out from behind." I shoved my chair away from the table and stood. "I still want to take my walk, Mack. I'm sure I'll see you again." I took a five out of my pocket and dropped it on the table.

"Wazzat?" Mack asked.

"That's awful good whiskey. I thought I'd pay for the bottle."

"Don't be an idjit. Billy Powers and his men don't pay for nothin' in Gila Bend. Not a goddamn thing—whores, booze, mercantile stuff, whatever. I'm ridin' a good Texas-made saddle that woulda cost me seventy-five, maybe eighty dollars. I jus' walked into the livery, seen her there, picked her up, unstrapped my old saddle and left it there on the ground, and fit the new one to my cayuse. Billy, he takes care of his boys."

"I'll keep that in mind," I said. "But I ain't one of Powers's men."

I left the saloon and continued my walk. All the businesses except the gin mills were closed. There were no kids playing in the street, no ol' gents sitting on benches whittling and arguing politics, no women scurrying about between the stores. It was as if some sort of plague had struck Gila Bend, wiping out all the good and normal people, leaving behind only the homicidal losers and kill-crazy gunmen. Come to think of it, that wasn't too far from actuality.

There was a light on inside a two-story hotel. I went in, got a first-floor room with a window looking out on the street, paid for three days, and stretched out on the bed, which wasn't half bad for a hotel bed. I was tired but couldn't sleep. The whiskey was still buzzing in my head and my conversation with Mack replayed in my mind. Finally, I said the hell with it, pulled on my boots and coat, and went back outside.

Down the street there was a gathering of thirty or forty men, clustered around two men on horses. As I got closer, I saw money was changing hands. I looked over the horses. One was a loud-colored Appaloosa that was well muscled and sleek and glowing with nervous sweat and mouthing his bit. The other was a tall black that looked to have some Thoroughbred blood. He was nicely put together. Both horses were studs—or, if not, they'd found interesting places to carry a couple doorknobs. The black was antsy and dancing a bit.

I like horse racing—always have. Covering ground real fast isn't all that important overall in a good horse, but still, racing was fun to watch. The cluster of men cleared back from the riders. The run was to be down the street to the end of the town, swing around the last building, and then race back to where they'd started. A fellow approached me with two-to-one odds on the black, but I'm not much of a wagering man and I declined.

The rider of the Appy was young, probably not twenty yet. The beard he was trying to grow was scrawny and didn't look like it was going to fill out anytime soon. He wore a holstered Colt. His hat looked new. The other rider was of the Billy Powers gang sort. He was at least half drunk, weaving slightly in his saddle.

They got their horses aligned and then held them on tight reins, both riders barely touching their horse's flanks with their heels. The kid wasn't wearing spurs, but the other had those sharp-roweled Mexican gutrippers tied onto his boots. That he used the spurs often was easy enough to see; the black's flanks were masses of healing cuts, scars, and some fresh slashes that were still weeping blood.

The moon had risen—a full one, casting a good deal of light. Other than that, the only illumination was that from the saloons. Both horses were dancing a bit, still on a tight rein.

"C'mon, goddammit!" the older rider shouted. "I ain't gonna sit out here all night."

A man stepped out of the crowd holding his pistol over his head. "On three when I fire," he shouted. "One . . . Two . . ." The black was in motion the very smallest bit of time before the starter yelled "three" and fired into the air.

Every man there saw the black jump the start. No one said a word about it.

Both horses knew their jobs well. They came off the start as if they were running from Satan himself, hurling clods of dirt behind them with all four hooves.

It took the Appaloosa only a half dozen long, powerful strides to catch the black—but he couldn't pass him. Or the kid was savvier than he looked and was holding his mount back, saving some horse for the run home.

Most—in fact, all—the races I've seen in Texas, the horse and rider automatically lose if the rider uses a quirt or crop in front of the saddle cinch. Apparently, that rule didn't apply in Gila Bend.

The outlaw was whipping hell out of his horse—in front of the cinch—for no reason at all. That black horse was running his heart: he didn't need the quirt or the cruel spurs to urge more speed out of him.

It was difficult to see what was going on because of the thick cloud of grit and dust behind them. I barely saw the outlaw raise his quirt and swing it at either the Appy or his rider. Several men who'd picked it up too laughed.

"Ol' Frankie, he don't like to lose," one said.

It was in that turn that the kid and the Appaloosa grabbed the lead. He turned smoothly and easily—as if he were on tracks. The black scrambled in the turn, shaking his head, long strands of foamy spittle flailing back from his muzzle as he ran. A bottle was passed around; there'd be nothing to see until the horses rounded the other end of town and hauled for home. I refused the drink and passed the whiskey on.

I had a real sick feeling about this horse race, and I wished I weren't there. Better yet, I wished neither the kid nor his hot Appaloosa were there.

The report of a pistol on the prairie is a flat *pop*. A shotgun is something completely different. There's a big *boom* that echoes about before it dies. The only thing louder than a shotgun is a Sharps or a Springfield.

I should have left right then—after I heard the deep bellow of a shotgun. I hadn't seen a scatter gun on the outlaw's saddle, but that didn't mean it wasn't there. It could have been a cutoff sheathed tight to the saddle fender or in or under his bedroll.

After a few moments, the outlaw loped his sweated black around the far end of town and came to us.

The kid walked out of an alley between a couple of buildings. I was pleased to see that—it's easy enough to kill a horse, I guess, and I was glad the kid walked out onto the street.

He strode up to the man he'd raced against and slapped him across his face. There isn't much more demeaning to a man than to be slapped.

"You killed a horse that had a whole lot better breeding than you have, you piece of shit," the boy snarled.

The kid stood back, his hand right over the Colt he wore.

"Why, goddamn," the outlaw said. "We got us a real gunfighter here."

The kid backed up a half step. His right hand was an inch above his pistol. "You killed my horse," he said, "because he was faster'n your horse."

The outlaw stepped out a bit from the other men. "You think you can take me, boy?"

"I'll tell you what—either I can or I'll or die trying."

I stepped in front of the young kid and drew. I put a couple of slugs into the outlaw's chest and stepped over to him to make certain he was dead. He was.

"Look here, mister—this wasn't your fight. You got no right to step . . ."

"I'll tell you what boy: this piece of trash would have kept talking to you a bit and then when you were about to answer, he'd have killed you."

"I'm faster—"

"You're a whole lot stupider," I interrupted. "Fast isn't all that important: accuracy is—and so is knowing the tricks."

For the first time, the young man's emotion showed in his eyes. They glistened a bit, and he wiped them with the back of his hand. "He was a good horse." His voice cracked on the word "horse."

"I'm sure he was, boy. But you've got something to do right away: buy a horse at the livery and get the hell out of town. This group is ugly already, and if you give them a little more time and a little more whiskey, there's going to be a bucketful of trouble."

"But . . . but you were the one who gunned that man."

"Yeah. I was. But they won't see it that way—at least not completely. In their thinking you caused the race and you caused the outlaw's death. Go on, kid, beat it."

"I don't have any money to buy a . . ."

I gave him a fifty from my vest pocket. "You do now. Collect your tack from your Appy, buy a horse, and haul ass. Hear?"

"Yessir, I do. Thanks. I don't know why you're doing this."

" 'Why' doesn't matter. Just get moving."

He turned back toward the alley he'd cut through to collect his saddle, bridle, and gear.

The outlaws stood around their dead comrade, looking down at him as if they'd never seen a corpse before. There was as much emotion as there'd be if one scorpion died in a nest of them.

"Sumbitch cheated at cards, too," one outlaw said.

Another slapped at his shirt pocket. "Shit," he said. "I'm outta makins'. Luke, lemme have a smoke, will ya?"

I walked away from them and went back to my hotel. I'd figured at least one or two would have tried to avenge the man on his back in the street. No one did—no one gave a damn.

Chapter Two

I figured there was no sense in going back to my hotel. My nerves were wound too tight to sleep and I'd just writhe around on the bed listening to the street noises.

I crossed the street and thought I'd try one of the saloons I hadn't yet visited. It was pretty much like the last one, but this place had the distinction of a large poster of a nude woman behind the bar. I stepped up and ordered a beer and took a closer look at the poster. It was punctured in a couple dozen places with bullet holes.

There was a pretty good crowd. All the poker tables were filled, and men were waiting for someone to bust out and free up a seat. A half dozen or so whores were circulating, their false smiles and makeup that looked like they'd put it on with a trowel an attempt to hide their ages.

A prostitute in Texas is worn out and used up by the age of maybe thirty. After that, everything begins to sag a bit and the look in their eyes as they work a crowd is no longer sexy or appealing: it's desperate.

I pushed my nickel across the bar for my beer and took a sip. I was surprised that it was icy cold. Not many gin mills made enough money to have ice cut and stored for them, but damn—that coldness sure improved the flavor of the beer.

I heard yelling from the second story and looked up. A pair of men were swinging at each other, noses already bloodied, faces showing that they'd received some hard blows. Finally, one fellow slammed his opponent in the gut with a round-house right that sent the men through the railing above the second floor. He tumbled to his side as he fell, arms waving. He landed on a poker table, smashing hell out of it in an eruption of cards, money, beer, and whiskey.

The bartender was a big man and didn't appear to be at all agile, but he surprised me by planting one hand on the bar and vaulting over it in a smooth, clean motion. He grabbed the guy who'd taken the dive by the back of the collar and the back of his denim pants and launched him a solid ten feet directly through the batwings—headfirst.

I found it odd that the only people who showed any interest in the fracas were me and the bartender. But I guess I need to add the whore who was outside and about to push open the batwings when the fist fighter opened them with his head. She went down like she'd been hit by a canon ball, sprawled out on the dirt and horseshit of the street.

There's a strange phenomena about cussing: it sounds logical and normal coming from a man, but from a woman—even a beat-up old whore—it jangles a fellow, makes him sort of cringe inside himself. The woman who got slammed by the flying outlaw was a fine example. Of course, I'd heard all the words before, so it wasn't that. I think it was a couple of things. For one, she hooked and threaded the words and phrases together in a manner I'd never heard before, juxtaposing the outlaw's parentage with his sex activities. Secondly, it was a sad thing to watch her do it. I'm not sure why that was true, but it was.

The piano player in the joint was good. Rather than rattling off a repetitious and boring series of the standards such as "Buffalo Gals," "Oh, Suzanna," and "When Johnny Comes Marching Home," this fellow had some genuine skill at the keyboard. I turned to face him, hooked a heel over the bar rail and watched and listened. I ordered another beer and would have liked a taste of that good whiskey I'd had during my talk with Mack, but doubted that I'd get anything other than the swill served to the general customers—redeye that tended to give a man the blind staggers and a hangover that made death welcome.

I was sucking my beer and enjoying the music when a sudden silence settled in the saloon. The piano player kept playing, but conversations at the poker tables and around the bar stopped for a moment, and all eyes swung toward the batwings. Mine joined them.

The man who had just entered must have been Billy Powers. Nobody in his right mind would dress as this fellow was dressed—not unless he had plenty of followers, and a very fast gun.

He wore an oversize Stetson that he must have had custom made, and from beneath it flowed a cascade of shoulder-length blond hair in the style of George Custer. His face was clean shaved and composed of angles: a somewhat prominent jaw, tight skin over sharp cheekbones, and lips that were thin, straight lines. He was maybe 5' 10" and carried a small roll of flab around his waist. He was wearing a buckskin coat with long fringes hanging from the sleeves. His shirt—white, with pearl buttons—was tucked into the waist of a pair of white pants. His boots were highly shined.

He carried a pair of Colts, tied low on his legs so that his fingertips fell naturally to the butts. Three men crowded in after him and placed themselves in positions to defend him—one on each side and one in front. There was nothing fancy about their apparel. They were everyday thugs.

The conversations picked up where'd they'd left off, but were quieter, more subdued. Powers strode over to the bar and with a slight motion of his head sent the fellow who'd been standing next to me scurrying away.

"My name is Billy Powers," he said. "I own this town."

I met his pale blue eyes. "My name is Pound Taylor," I said. "I don't own much of anything."

"You used to ride with Zeb Stone, right?"

I nodded.

"A good man, Zeb. We palled around as young bucks. Ol' Zeb could shoot, even back then. One of the fastest, most accurate pistol men I ever came across."

"He could shoot," I said.

"He was killed robbing a bank, right? And you was with him. How'd you get out of jail? Word I heard was that you were going to be strung up."

"Some friends busted me out," I said. "Actually, they were Zeb's relatives—two brothers and his father."

The bartender had hustled over with a bottle of that good whiskey and a pair of glasses and set them on the bar between Powers and me.

"Care for a drink?"

"Don't mind if I do," I said. I filled my shot glass as well as Powers's.

Powers slammed his; I sipped at mine, enjoying that fine smoky flavor.

"Some folks say you're a 'slinger, Pound. Is that true?"

"Hired gun? Hell, no. I can take care of myself and I've been lucky so far."

Powers poured us each another shot. "Ya know," he said, "there's probably a dozen men right here in this saloon who could leave you bleedin' in the streets after a fair, man-to-man gunfight."

"Wonderful. I'm happy for them." I poured my shot down and pushed away from the bar.

Two of the outlaws who'd come in with Powers were rapidly in front of me.

"That's real cute," Powers said. "You got a mouth

on you that's gonna get you killed one day, Pound."

"Maybe," I said. I had no more chance of getting through the two outlaws than I had of holding a stick of dynamite and touching off the fuse without being blown to hell. One already had his pistol unholstered, and the other's hand was on the grips of his weapon. And, there were Powers's Colts to clean up if I somehow made it through his men.

I turned back to the bar. "What is it you want from me, Powers?"

"Well, I'll tell you," he said. "See, my boy here, Jacob, is real fast with his Colt an' accurate enough to shoot the hair off a tick's nuts at a hundred yards." Powers nodded toward the man who hadn't yet drawn. He inhaled a deep breath and went on. "I figured matching you an' Jacob, here, would make a good contest. Here you are a shootist an' bank robber an' killer. An' Jacob, he's like a hound looking for a bitch in heat to test himself against. Maybe he isn't near as good as he thinks he is—or I do, for that matter. Seems to me, you two boys facin' one another would settle things out. Ya know?"

"I'm not a gunslinger, Powers. If your cretin friend here is looking for trouble, he needs to go somewhere else. Gunfights aren't circuses."

" 'Cretin'—that means dumb, right?"

"Yeah. It does. And any man who goes into a gunfight to please his boss is as stupid as a bucket of piss."

Powers laughed and took a step to his side. Jacob filled the spot Powers had left. Jacob was tall and appeared to be in his early twenties. His face was comely; he apparently hadn't been in the outlaw life long enough for it to leave its mark. His eyes were black, oily looking, intense, and they met and held mine. He smelled of pomade and bay rum.

"Seems to me you got no choice here, gunman. You're gonna fight me whether you like it or not. If you won't draw, I'll put a couple of rounds in your gut an' while you're bleedin' to death, I'll carve a notch in the grip of my pistol. So, like I said, you got no choice in the matter."

I smiled. "Come on, Jacob—do you go by Jake?— there's no reason for us to fight. Hell, we don't even know each other. It'd be plain silly for one of us to end up dead just to give your boys a show."

I picked up the bottle of whiskey, took a shot glass from behind the bar, filled it, and pushed it in front of Jacob. "Let's have a drink and talk a bit."

The outlaw's eyes showed quick confusion, which is exactly what I was looking for. I put my right arm over Jacob's shoulders like an old friend—then grabbed the back of Jacob's head and smashed it facedown onto the bar. The snap of cartilage was loud and distinct, not unlike a dry stick breaking. Blood gushed from each nostril. I pulled the kid's head back by his hair and crashed it into the bar again. Jacob, unconscious, crumpled to the floor.

I drew, my Colt trained on Billy Powers's chest.

Powers, for his part, was laughing loudly. "Goddamn!" he roared. "If you ain't a hardcase, I guess I never seen one," and broke into laughter again.

Several of Powers's men had drawn their weapons; Powers shut them down with a desultory wave. "Git Jacob outta here," he said. "He's messin' up the nice clean floor of this fine establishment."

Powers paused for a moment. "How about holstering that Colt, Pound? Makes me a bit edgy to have the sumbitch pointed at me. Nervouslike, ya know?"

"I lower my gun and your boys fill me with holes? No thanks."

"No. Shit, no. I already waved them off. We'll have a drink is all, an' then you go on your way. You got my word on that as a Son of the Confederacy."

"How do I know your word is worth a cow flop, Powers?"

"I guess you gotta gamble on that."

"Yeah. I guess I do." After an excruciatingly long few moments, I holstered the Colt.

Powers poured us each a shot. "You woulda shot Jacob's ass clean off," he said. "Damn fool has been snortin' around like a elk at rutting time, looking to prove he was a fast gun. He ain't bad, but he's stupid. An' stupid gets more men killed than fast."

The piano started up again, poker games were

resumed, and the noise level in the saloon returned to its normal raucous sounds.

"Grab the bottle an' let's go on back to my office where we can talk," Powers said. "The racket in here's nuff to drive a man loopy."

"Office?" I asked.

"Well, hell's bells, it's just a little room, really. I have one in each of the joints in Gila Bend."

I followed Powers to the end of the bar. He opened the door, reached back, and grabbed a lamp from a hook on the wall, leaving the four men who were playing poker at the table under the lamp essentially with no light. Not one of the four said a word; not a single one even looked up.

It was a fairly small room—perhaps twelve feet square with a couple raggedy stuffed chairs and a table from the bar. Powers waved me to a chair. He sat behind the table. I set the bottle on the table in front of us and he took a couple of tumblers from a little shelf behind him and poured a solid three inches into each.

"I noticed you picked up the bottle with your left hand," Powers said. "An' I noticed your pistol is on your right side."

I shrugged, as if the whole thing was of no significance, and picked up a glass—with my left hand. "A man either learns some habits or gets killed," I said. "I do the right-hand, left-hand stuff without thinking about it."

Powers grinned a wolf's grin. "What would you say if I told you I had a 12-gauge taped real nice under this table, aimed at you square on?"

"Well, I'll tell you. I can't draw and fire faster than you can pull a trigger on your 12-gauge. What I can do is this: watch your shoulders, your eyes, the way you're breathing. Are you sucking little clumps of air like you're ready to make a move?

"If it was time, I'd roll off this chair and plant at least one .45 in your head. 'Course it's possible—hell, likely—you could see my move and cut loose with your scatter gun. Either way, we'd just be trading lives—and that doesn't make much sense to me. But if that's what you need, let's do it."

Powers laughed. "You sure got everythin' all figured out, ain't you?"

I didn't answer.

"Might be possible I could use a man like you, Pound." There was no more laughter in his voice. He was talking business.

"Know this, Powers," I said. "I'd a whole lot prefer to be in hell with a toothache and a white-hot iron stuck up my ass." I snorted derisively. "Jesus. Backing down ribbon clerks and sodbusters and scaring women in town and taking things from the gin mills an' the mercantile without paying for them isn't the way I go. That's chickenshit stuff. You know that, and so do I."

Powers stood. "Listen here now . . ." he began.

"See, Powers, you're not quite as bright as you think you are. You stood up and away from the 12-gauge and you must know I'm faster than you and I could send you to hell in a hair of a second."

"You *think* you . . ."

"It's not what I think, it's what I know. I could put five rounds in your chest and head before you cleared leather."

"Go ahead an' do it, then. I don't give a good goddamn about nothin' since Bobby Lee handed over the Confederacy at Appomattox." The words had the taste of a schoolyard dare.

Powers touched a raw and open cut on me. "Look, I fought for the Confederacy. We waited for a good chance to shut down the Northern Aggressors. Gettysburg could have done it—and if we'd taken that, Washington was next, and the whole goddamn war would have been over. It didn't turn out that way, though."

"No, it didn't. But that's funny—Gettysburg was right where I parted company with the Rebel Army. I heard about Lee's plan to take that cemetery hill, and it was not only stupid, it was flat-out crazy. I grabbed me a good horse and lit out an' never looked back."

"Sounds like you're proud to be a deserter."

"I'm neither proud nor ashamed—neither one. It's somethin' that happened. I didn't care to die there, so I left."

I didn't answer. I turned and walked out of the room leaving the door open. The bedlam in the saloon was more than I could take after my talk with Powers, so I walked on through and out the batwings, again followed by a cloud of smoke and stink.

Even outdoors there was cacophony in Gila Bend. I watched as two drunken thugs arranged a horse race down the length of the town. Several others stood around, money moving from one hand to another.

Both horses looked good—far better than the crowbait I'd seen Powers's men riding. Both horses dug out from the start and were in a full gallop in three strides. They were evenly matched, and both appeared to have a ton of heart and desire to win this race. They passed me head-to-head and running hard—at least until one of the riders decided to better his odds a bit. He reached over, grabbed his opponent's shirt, and dragged him off his horse.

Some of the crowd laughed and cheered; the men who'd bet on the fallen rider started swinging, gouging, and kicking. I'd read one time about sharks in a feeding frenzy and how they often tore pieces out of other sharks as well as their prey. That's what this kick-ass looked like—a fighting frenzy. I watched for a few minutes, then headed back to my hotel. As I picked up my key at the desk, gunfire broke out on the street.

It was stiflingly hot in my room, and although the window was wide open, there was no breeze. I took off my boots, stretched out on my bed, and gave the last couple of days some thought—which led to some other thoughts and memories.

What the hell am I doing in this hellhole? Powers is just as likely to backshoot me as not. I could gather up my horse, ride out, dig up my money, and keep right on going. But I didn't.

I guess I've always been like that. Any

challenge—even a perceived challenge that was unstated but nevertheless there—was something I couldn't refuse. I saw myself at age eleven getting my ass kicked around behind the schoolhouse by a sixteen-year-old farm boy who'd knocked my books out of my hand. I knew I didn't have a chance against this kid, but I laid into him, and we did a lot of rolling around in the dirt cussin' at each other until the kid's size and strength took over. I had a hell of a shiner and a broken tooth, but I hadn't backed down, and that was more important to me than a little pain.

I sighed aloud.

It was the same thing with the War of Northern Aggression. I was dead sure the South would go down: we were outnumbered, outgunned, outsupplied, and most of our officers had the soft hands of men who'd never chopped wood or followed a mule's ass over acre after acre of land, keeping the plow blade steady and perfectly in line.

Most of the Northern troops were working men, mainly farmers. They were tough and hardy and their leaders were clever and intelligent. We won some skirmishes and some battles, too, but even when we did, the Yankees came after us. It was a losing proposition.

So why am I here in Gila Bend? There'd been no challenge. The town was a cesspool full of murderers, rapists, whores, gamblers, and general lunatics who liked the smell of blood. Why was I still here?

I sighed again and never did come up with an answer that made any sense.

I drifted off to sleep and awakened early. I had breakfast at the hotel restaurant and walked down to the livery to fetch my horse. He was looking good: the liveryman had polished him up real nice with a soft brush, and it was obvious he was feeding the animal well. I tacked up the horse and rode down the street and out of Gila Bend. The mercantile owner was just opening his place and a fat man, yawning hugely, was fitting a key to the door of the assay office.

My good bay horse was frisky in the relative cool of the morning. He cow-hopped a few times and shook his head, trying to get under the bit and burn off some of his excess energy. I let him play but easily kept him under control. I'd have liked to let him run for a mile or so, but the area was too heavy on prairie dog holes to risk it. Instead, I held him to a slow lope.

The land around Gila Bend isn't what you'd call pretty. It's rocky in some places and there are stands of scraggly desert pines, but for the most part, it's a haven for rattlesnakes and prairie dogs and the critters they feed on. There's nowhere near enough buffalo grass to keep weight on beef. But it's quiet—that's one thing it has going for it.

I'd been riding for half an hour or so when I turned in my saddle and looked behind me, a habit I developed long ago. I was putting a good bit of dust in the air, but so was the rider a mile or so behind me. The dust pointed at him like an accusing finger.

Since I had no particular destination in mind, I swerved sharply to my left and let my horse have a bit more rein. The rider behind me made the same turn, making it clear that he was doggin' me rather than going somewhere. That made me kinda curious—and kinda nervous, too. If he was out after me, he'd been within rifle range, and if he was a decent shot, he'd have picked me off. Still, I felt the hairs on the back of my neck rise as I rode, and that's not usually a good sign.

There was a group of trees around a little water hole not too far ahead. I scanned them carefully, seeking a specific type of branch. As soon as I saw it, I heeled my horse into a gallop, directly at the trees. We approached like a runaway locomotive. I kicked my boots out of my stirrups and tied my reins together. The branch was coming at me real fast, but I was ready.

After all, I had practiced this move with my boyhood pals hour after hour, getting quite proficient at it.

I had to reach a bit higher than I wanted to as my horse thundered under the limb, but I got both hands on it and let my own momentum swing me up until I was bent over it. I adjusted myself in a sitting position on the limb. The other rider came tear-assing after me and I dropped onto his back, taking both of us to the ground, with him absorbing most of the impact. It was Jacob, the fellow whose face I'd slammed against the bar the night before.

The wind had been knocked out of him, but I was fine. I scrambled away from him and stood, watching him trying to suck air.

"You don't learn real fast," I said, when he was finally breathing almost normally. His nose was bleeding again. After a bit, he stood.

"Powers send you, or you out here on your own?"

"Some of each," he answered, his voice sounding like that of a man with a bad nose or a sinus infection or some damned thing. "Billy told me to follow you out—see where you was goin'. He said if I killed you, it wouldn't break his heart, but that was up to me."

I'd already moved my coat behind the grips of my Colt. "No good reason for you to die out here, boy," I said, "and that's what's going to happen if you draw on me."

The damned fool had already set himself in what he thought was a good gunfighting position, his body turned slightly sideways, one boot a foot behind the other. I watched his eyes. When they told me he was going to make his move, I let him get ahold of his pistol and then I drew and shot him three times center-chest. He was probably dead before he hit the ground.

I walked out to fetch my horse. He'd never given me any trouble in walking up to him in a pasture, and I didn't expect any now. I was right; he was cropping grass a couple hundred yards beyond the trees. I climbed on, and we fetched the young fellow's horse and went back to where the corpse lay. He had a rope on his saddle, which made things easier for me. I hefted him across the seat of his saddle, arms hanging on one side, legs on the other. I tied him down nice and tight with his lariat, mounted my horse, and took the reins to the other. He followed docilely enough as we headed back to Gila Bend. I dropped his reins when we were a mile or so out. He slowed a bit but continued to follow. I figured he had a stall somewhere in town, and that's where he'd head. I stopped and when the corpse-burdened horse drew up next to us I gave him a sound whack on the rump and he picked up his pace to his home—wherever that may have been.

It was still early when I turned my horse back into the livery and headed for a saloon. All that time out in the sun, breathing more dust than air, had given me a powerful thirst.

There were only a few hard-core drinkers at the bar at that time of the morning, but there were a couple of poker games going on at the tables. The men playing cards looked like they'd been there at least all night: they were red-eyed, their voices crusty with endless cigars and cigarettes, and they were totally silent as they played.

All of them looked at me as I came in, and then, instead of looking away, they held their eyes on me. Jacob's horse had apparently gotten to town, just as I expected him to.

"Beer," I said to the bartender.

He fiddled nervously with the bar rag in his hands. "Look, maybe it'd be good for you to go across the street or to one of the other saloons," he said.

Well, hell. "Beer," I repeated, a bit more forcefully.

The 'tender drew a schooner, used his flat stick to whisk the excess foam and set the drink in front of me. He started to turn away.

"Wait a minute," I said. "You got some trouble with me, not wanting me to drink in your joint?"

He turned back, his face reddening. "Goddamn right," he said. "Sending Billy's man back over his saddle is gonna cause some trouble. I don't want that trouble here. I lose enough goddamn money giving booze and beer away to Powers's boys."

"Why do you do it, then?"

The bartender shook his head in disgust. I didn't know if it was my question that brought about his displeasure or the admission he'd just made. Maybe it was a combination of the two.

"You think I got a choice? I ain't. When Powers first came to Gila Bend he demanded free drinks for him an' his men down to the joint on the corner by the empty lot. The 'tender—a friend of mine—told Billy to go to hell." He poured himself a shot and dumped it down.

"We found that bartender hanging from a limb on the tree near where the church used to be before it was burned. They'd strung him up and then used him for target practice. There wasn't a whole lot left of him."

I nodded. The barkeep went to the far end of his bar, putting as much distance as he could between us. I finished my beer and called for another. He fetched it quickly, put it in front of me, grabbed the empty mug, and damn near ran to the far end of the bar.

I heard the batwings open but didn't need to look up to see who was coming in. The looks on the faces of all the others there answered that question for me. I eased my coat behind the grips of my Colt and turned.

Billy Powers was wearing that same ridiculous white suit. He stood there, maybe fifteen feet away, motionless, not speaking, his eyes hard—like those of a snake that'd backed its prey into a corner. We held eye contact for a long time. I took a half step away from the bar.

After a long, long moment, Powers strode over to stand next to me. He motioned to the 'tender, who set a bottle and a shot glass on the bar. Powers poured, drank, and poured again. I'd turned to face him.

He went through some facial contortions and then he laughed—hard and long. "Goddamn," he said. "You got a set of eggs on you sendin' my boy back over his saddle."

I watched Powers's right hand as he spoke and laughed and snorted.

I saw in Dodge City not more than a couple of years ago a laughing, apparently drunk man put his right arm over the shoulders of a man who had been an enemy for years. The jolly fellow had a stiletto up his sleeve and he used it like a surgeon, reaching his hand around to quickly and quite easily slash the neck of the other man. He'd laughed as he saw his enemy's life spilling out his throat.

Powers eventually settled down. He leaned over the bar, picked up a shot glass and put it in front of me, then reached for the bottle.

I said, "Thanks, but no thanks."

"C'mon, Pound. A little morning bracer is good for the heart an' bowels an' so forth."

So is a morning .45 slug.

"No thanks," I said again.

"I'll be damned if you ain't a strange one," Powers said. "You don't want to ride with me an' my boys, you ain't played no cards, you sure as hell ain't no miner, an' you haven't mounted a single whore. An' on top of that all you gunned one of my men and rode on back to town like you was out picking daisies for your ma. What the hell you doin' here?"

Good question: what the hell am I doing here?

"Someone real soon would have fed lead to your Jacob—if not me, then someone else. I'm afraid the dumb sumbitch has been reading too many of them dime novels. An' why am I here? Well, I'll tell you, Billy Powers—simply 'cause I want to be. When I don't want to be here any longer, I'll ride out and go on my way."

Powers was no longer playing the congenial buffoon. His face was tight. "You know," he said, "one day you an' me is goin' at it—one to one."

I grinned. "Could well be, Billy, but not right now, not on this day. This beer is tastin' awfully good. Maybe one day we'll have somethin' to battle over, but not now."

"You pulling the cork on one of my men ain't somethin' to battle about?"

I shook my head. "No. Maybe if he was your ramrod or had some value in your crew but not Jacob. I just happened to be the first in line to take out the mouthy little bastard."

"I can't argue that—the kid ran his mouth a lot. But still, you gunned one of my men."

"True. I did just that."

"I can't let that go by, Pound."

"OK," I said, as I set my mug on the bar. "Let's get to it, then."

Powers seemed to think it over. "Even if you got real lucky and took me down, my men would . . ."

"Let's cut the shit," I said. "The scum you ride with are along for the free booze, the power, the free whores, all that. I doubt there's one of them who'd come to me after I killed you, or even give a damn. No?"

"Maybe. Thing is, you think can beat me, drop me. You're wrong."

My old way of moving my coat behind my holster kicked in like a bad habit. "No, Billy," I said. "You can't beat me. You can beat your whores, you can beat the folks who live in Gila Bend, and you can beat the scum and losers you ride with. But you got no more chance of walking away from a gunfight with me than you do jumpin' over the godddam moon."

Powers finished his drink and left the saloon. After a minute or so, the poker games picked up where they'd left off, and a couple of drifter types came in and stood at the bar. It was, once again, business as usual.

I was still a little antsy, and I continued my walk around Gila Bend. All in all, it didn't seem like a bad town. If Powers could be eliminated, the town would probably grow, get a school, more businesses, all that. I turned into the mercantile. A fussy little baldheaded fellow hustled over and asked if I needed help finding anything. I told him I didn't; I was just looking.

There's something about a mercantile that's always appealed to me. It could be the scent. The smells of good, oiled leather; the steely metallic farm tools and plows; the barrels of apples; the bolts of cloth; and even the penny candy mixed in the air in a pleasant, comfortable cloud.

The store was well-equipped. I stood in front of the handgun case and looked over the stock, noting that there was no army junk for sale; Colt predominated. The saddles were fine ones, with precise stitching, assembled from excellent-grade leather that gave off the scent of neat's-foot oil. The prices were somewhat dear, but the saddles were a type that would outlast a man—even a young man—if he took decent care of it.

I took an apple from the barrel and munched as I walked up and down the aisles. Finally, after seeing everything, I went over to the counter. There was a glass jar of cheroots on display, and I took a couple.

"How much do I owe you?" I asked the nervous storekeeper.

He looked surprised. "Oh! I thought you were . . . well, anyway, that'll be twelve cents."

I paid and went back out onto the street. There was a wagon parked in front at the hitching rail; I fed the core of the apple to the horse.

I walked a bit farther after the mercantile and found myself in front of the burned-out shell of the sheriff's office. The door was hanging from one hinge. I pushed it lightly with my boot, and it collapsed inward with what sounded like a sigh of relief. It was safe enough to walk into the place since there was no chance of falling through the floor. It didn't have a floor as such; it'd been on leveled ground.

The office was as much a mass of charred wood and papers as it was the first time I'd seen it. There were a bunch of brass cartridge casings on the floor. Whoever was defending the office didn't go down easy or without a big fight—that was clear.

There was a group of Wanted posters on the floor, and on some of them parts of the text were still legible. I paged through them and was somewhat disappointed when I didn't find one that cited me.

It was a good goddamn shame about the tipped and burned rolltop desk. It was easy to see that it was once a quality piece, with the wood dove-tailed rather than nailed or glued.

I often think that if I hadn't become a teacher, a drunk, and a bank robber, I might have gone into carpentry and furniture making. There's a very real something powerful and good that clings to a quality piece of work, be it a chair or desk or table or barn, that holds to the product and will do so until it's destroyed.

There's a simple beauty in the work, too: the cutting, the sanding, the joining of parts are straightforward, and the maker always puts his name somewhere on the finished piece. A bank robber or a killer doesn't sign his work.

"Ahhh, shit," I said aloud.

I walked back through the burned-out door and doorway that led to the two cells. Fire doesn't do much to cold rolled steel. The bars probably looked as good as they ever had. There was a scorched slop bucket in one cell, along with what had probably been a meal tray.

There was also a skeleton jammed into the corner of the cell. Of course, much of the flesh had burned away, and rats and other vermin stripped off the rest. The hairless skull had fallen forward and rested on its side on the floor, eye holes watching me. Some of the longer bones—the long leg and arm bones—had been wrenched free and carried away, no doubt by dogs and, possibly, coyotes.

I moved on to the second of the two cells. There

was no skeleton in that one—it was empty except for yet another scorched slop bucket.

The cells reminded me of the days and hours I spent in similar ones, awaiting my date with the hangman. That was a few years ago, but the sensations and memories still sent a chill down the length of my spine. Being killed in a gunfight or while robbing a bank wouldn't bother me much—such deaths are quick and unforeseeable. But Jesus, I could see the gallows through my cell window and the waiting was the worst part of the whole package. I left the building, crunching over the door to the street that had fallen in. It was good to be outside.

"Kinda like it in there, do ya?" a voice called to me from the street. Calvin, the bar-rag I'd discussed Gila Bend with when I first came to town, walked a bit unsteadily.

"Can't say I do."

"There's some history in that ol' jail," Calvin said. "Maybe you want to hear about it?"

"Maybe."

Calvin cleared his throat. "A day like this, why it's just natural for a man to develop a thirst— wouldn't you say so?"

I sighed. "C'mon," I said, and went to a gin mill across the street. Some folks looked up when I walked in and stood at the bar. The fellow next to me looked around and then said surreptitiously, "You done good. The more of them snakes gets killed, the fewer there'll be."

I guess it doesn't take news at all long to find its way into every bar in town.

I bought a bottle of rotgut and a couple schooners of beer and sat at a table at the rear, my back to the wall. Calvin hustled through the batwings and joined me. He pulled the cork on the bottle and began sucking at it without benefit of a glass. He brought the level of the bottle down close to three inches.

"Kinda under the weather today." He grinned. "A little bracer'll fix me right up." He took a long drink from his beer and grunted contentedly. "Well," he began, "maybe you heard that there've been four lawmen killed off since Billy Powers rode in."

"Yeah. I heard that somewhere."

"The first one Billy got in a tussle with had been in office a few years—a good man. Handy with a pistol an' a rifle an' put up with no shit in his town, I'll tell you that. Billy met him right out on the street. The sheriff was fast; Billy was faster. By then, folks was scared of Billy and nobody admitted to seeing nothing."

Calvin sucked at the whiskey again. "The second one was but a kid, maybe twenty-four or twenty-five. Nice enough fella, but he didn't have no place in that office. One morning he set out to serve a warrant someplace or another and was picked off his horse with a buffalo gun. Sumbitch left a hole in him big enough to drive a freighter through.

"The third one was a long time coming. Word

had got around that Gila Bend wasn't healthy for lawmen. He wasn't in town a week before somebody blew the hell out of him with a scatter gun—both barrels, I heard—as he was walkin' out of the mercantile.

"This last fella was a hellcat. Whipcord tough, smart as a goddamn fox, and hotter'n hell with a pistol. One of Billy's men tried to take him down one night, and the lawmen emptied his pistol into the outlaw. That there must have pissed Billy off no little bit. A couple-three nights later, Billy and his entire goddamn crew attacked the sheriff in his office. From the sound of the gunfire, a man would think he was hearin' the battle of Shiloh all over again." Calvin poured a few inches of whiskey into his half-full schooner and swirled the mixture with a grubby finger.

"The sheriff had him a couple of rifles, a scatter gun, an' his pistol. The fight went on for half the night 'til a half dozen of Billy's boys flung torches through the windows. The place went up like a stack of hay. The sheriff didn't have no choice but to get the hell out—it was that or burn to death, an' I guess the lawman preferred a bullet or two to the fire. He got put down 'fore he was two full steps outta the office. There was a drunk in one cell. He burned up with the office."

We were both silent for a few moments. Then Calvin said, "So that's her—the story of Gila Bend. Ain't been nobody interested in takin' the job since, an' I can't say I blame them. Hell, it's like committin' suicide." Calvin set his empty mug on the table. "Say, you wouldn't care to buy me another beer, would you?"

"No. Keep the whiskey." I pushed my chair back and stood. "Thanks for the information."

I went back to my hotel, the taste of the beer sour in my throat and mouth. I sat out in front and put a match to one of my cheroots. It was a good smoke—seemed fresh, and tasted good.

Why the hell am I still here in this goddamn garbage pit? All I gotta do is get my horse, fetch my money from its hiding place, and ride on.

Gila Bend was no concern of mine—none at all. So why was I still here?

Chapter Three

I sat out in front of the hotel for a good bit longer, at least until the heat became really oppressive. I generally don't mind hot weather—and if a man does mind it, he'd best stay the hell out of West Texas.

I've always enjoyed watching streets and the activity on them. There wasn't much in Gila Bend to watch, so when a fellow in a nicely fitting dark suit and polished boots rode by on an obviously well-bred horse, I paid more attention to him than I would to other passersby. One thing I noticed even before the suit and the sleek strength of his horse was the fact that he was wearing a derby—not a Stetson or Stetson-type hat.

I figured that if he was thinking about going into any of the saloons, he might want to leave the hat with his horse. No one but a dude would wear a silly lid like a derby, and I doubted that Billy Powers and his crew were real friendly to greenhorns who belonged in Boston much more than they did in Gila Bend.

Once, a few years back, in a cattle town called

Divinity, I saw a dude get a foot shattered by a .45 slug. A bunch of drunks had decided to make him dance by shooting as close as possible to his feet. One cowhand was a bit too sauced to aim, and he shot the poor fellow's foot. I could easily see that happening here. It didn't, though. The town was as quiet as a graveyard at midnight.

By and by I was developing quite a thirst. Having cold beer available was spoiling me; in the overwhelming majority of towns, beer was served piss warm.

I'd been in each of the five saloons in Gila Bend, and they were all the same except the one that had the piano player who could play more than two or three songs—and play them well. I walked over to that one. There were drinkers and card players, but at that time of day—midafternoon—it didn't smell quite as bad as usual inside. I stood at the bar and ordered a beer. I'd often wondered why the gin mills didn't provide stools for the bar drinkers to sit on as they drank. I'd finally figured it out: a stool was easy to pick up and easy to swing, and if swung with enough power, easy to break. With the number of fights in most saloons, the owner'd go broke buying stools.

I lit another cheroot and made a mental note to buy more of them—perhaps a boxful if the mercantile had enough in stock. I drank my beer unhurriedly, kinda savoring it. Below the mandatory nude over the bar was a somewhat battered mirror that was a brownish yellow color from the smoke it was forced to endure. It was my habit to be aware of what was happening behind me, particularly in a place like Gila Bend.

The dude I'd seen earlier walked in, minus his derby, and strode up to the bar.

"Afternoon, sir," he said.

I nodded. I was having a fine time; I didn't need some clown to talk at me.

"I believe," he went on, "that you're Lawrence Basil Taylor. Am I not correct?"

"No, you're not. My name is Pound and I wonder if you could find someone else to pester, 'cause I don't have the time or the interest to flap gums with you."

"Here's how I heard the name Pound," the dude said, as if he hadn't heard my surly response. "You were teaching school in some broken-down little burg, and you ordered up some things in the town mercantile. You signed the purchase form with *L.B. Taylor*. The moron clerk made the ridiculous assumption that Pound was you're your given name and you abbreviated it with the initials L.B., and from then on he—and the rest of the town—referred to you as Pound. You tended to get drunk and fall over at that time—in class or not. Correct? And then Zeb Stone came to town and the two of you became partners and you started robbing banks with him."

"Look," I said, "this is goddamn ridiculous. I don't have any idea what you're talking about, and I don't care to hear any more of it. You understand?"

"Certainly," he said. "First, let me show you this."

The dude reached into his coat pocket and took out a tightly folded document of some kind. "Please, Mr. Taylor, please listen to me. It's for your own good—I promise you that."

"Yeah," I said, "lots of legal documents are for the good of me and my neighbors—like the goddamn bank foreclosures and tax liens on farmland and so forth."

The dude grinned a bit. "Mr. Taylor," he said very placidly, as if we were discussing the price of corn, "this very document may well keep you alive."

"What? What's this all about?"

"I'll tell you—if you give me a chance."

"OK, tell me what you're after."

"Certainly. I'm the circuit rider—the judge—for these parts. I make a circuit and hear cases, decide on sentences, settle land disputes, and so forth."

"You've done a helluva job in Gila Bend," I said.

"Your sarcasm is well-founded, Mr. Taylor. I can't deny that. But here's my offer, signed by ol' Sam Houston himself: if you become the lawman in Gila Bend for a year—only a year—your robbery and murder charges will be totally extinguished."

"Lemme see that paper," I said. I read it carefully. It was precisely and exactly as the dude presented it, except, of course, it had a blank line where the outlaw agreeing to the proposition was to sign. Apparently it didn't matter what thief, outlaw, bank robber, or killer the judge signed on—the promise would apply.

I shook my head. "You think I'm a gunman, no? That I shoot people whenever I care to? Lemme tell you this: I've killed no one beyond a kid who challenged me, and a couple of folks in banks who were truly stupid. If anyone was to try to clean up Gila Bend, the street would run with blood."

"Isn't it true that when you chop a snake's head off, the rest of it dies, too?"

"So you want me to gun Billy Powers."

"No, not unless it comes to that. What I want is for you to cover the commitment set forth in the pardon—to be the law in Gila Bend for a full year."

"No. I won't do it."

The judge began refolding his precious document, but stopped when I said, "The problem is that you know where I am now. With a word from you, the bounty hunters and Rangers would swarm around me and kill me right then or string me up after a parody of a trial."

"All I can do is give you my word, Mr. Taylor. But I've made this offer to a couple of Butch Cassidy's men, as well as a hired gun out of Dodge and a half-breed named Small Bear—all wanted and all with good money on their heads. I gave them my word I wouldn't reveal a thing about my meeting with him. I've kept my word. I was able to convince them all except Small Bear, and him I shot and killed because he was preparing to kill me."

I looked down at the judge's waist—he wasn't wearing a gunbelt. There was no lump under either arm that would indicate a shoulder holster.

"How . . . ?"

The judge held out his right hand, there was a quiet metallic *click*, and a Derringer two-shot over and under magically appeared in his palm. "I made the device myself," he said. "It's spring loaded and quite simple, really. The Derringer rests just in front of my elbow. A certain motion of my arm releases the spring and shoves the pistol into my hand." He put the Derringer back under his shirt cuff and slid it up to his elbow and then straightened his shirt a bit. The weapon was completely invisible.

I couldn't help being impressed. "Damn," I said. "If that ain't somethin'."

"Yes. Well. I don't need a decision from you right now, Mr. Taylor. I'll be in Gila Bend a couple of days having my horse reshod and trying to make some sense out of this town and Billy Powers."

"You can't make sense where there is none," I said.

"Perhaps. Now, is my word that I'll release information about you to no one, ever, for any reason enough to keep me alive?"

I finished the beer in my mug and signaled the bartender for another. The judge stood quietly next to me, staring into the mirror. I thought for a bit.

"I've always figured I was a pretty fair judge of a man," I said. "I'll accept you at your word. But leave me the hell alone, hear?"

"Fine," the judge said. He turned away from me and walked out of the saloon.

The West is getting stranger and stranger. Judges offering to let off killers, lunatics taking over towns, half the Confederate Army real sure the war isn't over yet, every man from the age of ten carrying a sidearm. The buffalo herds have been cut by two-thirds by skin-hunters who set up on a knoll and pick off two-three dozen shaggies with a Sharps, skin 'em out, and leave the meat to rot. Railroads goin' all over the goddamn place. I dunno. It doesn't make sense.

I was getting awfully accustomed to sleeping in a bed and having my meals prepared for me. Even a dung heap like Gila Bend had its advantages—iced beer being one of them.

I spent a good deal of time sitting in front of my hotel, reading a newspaper or simply watching the street. I also spent a good deal of time bellied up to the bar with a foaming schooner in front of me. As I thought about it, I hadn't had a real break—a rest—since the day Zeb Stone and I robbed our first bank together a few years back. There were a slew of better towns and cities to rest up in, but they had the disadvantage of lawmen and bounty hunters. At least in Gila Bend I didn't need to worry about either.

I saw that judge every so often and nodded, but we didn't talk again. Every time I saw him, I thought about his ludicrous proposition. I'd make about as good a lawman as a rattlesnake would a house pet.

All around me Gila Bend went on as it had—gunfights in the streets, murders in the saloons, and normal folks who scurried when they had to be on the streets rather than walking normally or stopping to pass the time with a friend or neighbor.

One afternoon I was sitting in my usual rocker in front of the hotel when a kid—a boy of ten or so—came running down the street with a large, shaggy, brownish colored dog right at his heels. The kid pulled to a stop not too far from me and took a homemade ball from his pocket—a lumpy thing bound around and around with tape. The dog nearly jumped out of his skin, dancing in front of the kid, whining, pawing at him.

I'm not a sentimental man, but the love between the boy and his dog was palpable; I could feel it in the air.

The kid hurled the ball, and his dog took off like a racehorse, fetched it back after almost skidding by it, and dropped it at the boy's feet, tail beating so that his whole hind end wiggled. The boy wouldn't trade that mongrel dog for all the riches in the world.

He threw the ball again and the dog took off after it—just as a couple of Billy Powers's men rode out from the mouth of an alley. One of their horses spooked at the dog, and the rider cursed, drew, and shot the dog. The slug must have taken that good dog in the hip because his back legs didn't work, and he was dragging himself toward the ball with his forepaws. The outlaws laughed and then the second one drew and put a bullet into the dog's head. I vaulted over the rail in front of the hotel and shot him out of his saddle. The first rider, still wrestling a bit with his horse, began to take aim at me. I put a slug between his eyes.

The boy stood like a statue for a long moment, and then he ran to his dog. He cradled the dead animal in his lap like a mother holding a child, tears gushing from his eyes, the look on his face so stricken, so hurt, that I knew he'd never get over it. I walked over to him, ignoring the two corpses and the loose horses and crouched down next to him. "I'm real sorry, boy," I said. "Real sorry."

The kid said between gasps of anguish, "Rex, he was the best friend I ever had. And now . . ."

I straightened and walked over to the ball, picked it up, and brought it back to the boy. "You keep this ball, son, and you'll always have it to remind you of your dog—your best friend."

"I . . . I need to bury Rex," the boy said. He attempted to lift the dog, but he probably weighed a good hundred pounds and his master couldn't get him off the ground.

"You wait here," I said. "I'll fetch a cart from the livery and then we'll go to wherever you want to bury Rex."

I hustled to the livery, tossed a ten to the owner,

grabbed a manure shovel, and climbed into a cart someone had just returned. I swung around to the horrible tableau of the boy and his dead dog, and as I looked a spark was ignited somewhere deep inside me. It was like a tiny part of my brain was aflame—and that fire was spreading.

I had a lot of respect for that boy. His eyes were still running tears, but he wasn't about to let me hear him sob.

"Turn onto that wagon road up there," he said, after we'd gone a mile or so out of town. His voice was slightly shaky. "Over by them trees," he said.

I reined to a stop and the boy jumped out, took the shovel, and started to dig under a desert pine. After a while I said, "I'll spell you with the shovel."

"Don't need no help," was his response.

That boy dug for at least a full hour in the midday heat without slowing or stopping for a breather. He dug a hole about four feet deep and a couple wide. I jumped down and helped him get Rex out of the little wagon. Then he said, "You mind walkin' off a bit, mister? This is private stuff." I did that. When I saw him putting dirt back into the hole I went back to the cart.

"I guess I'll walk from here," he said. "Thanks for your help."

"Glad to give you a hand," I said.

He wasn't quite finished with what he had to say. Finally, he said, "Shootin' them two dirty sonsabitches was a good thing, mister. Rex was jus' chasin' his ball. He wasn't out to scare no horses."

"I know, boy."

"My name's Evan Murfin," he said. "My pa has a little farm an' he makes some whiskey, too. You ever need any kinda help, you come to my pa an' me, OK?"

"You bet."

Evan reached up to shake my hand. At first I thought his palm was merely sweaty, but then I saw blood dripping. He'd shoveled himself into blisters and then broke those and hit blood. It hadn't slowed him down. He turned away and began walking. I turned the cart back toward Gila Bend. As I watched the boy walk, the fire in my mind was growing. I saw the whole scene over again: the joy of Evan and his dog, the outlaw's first shot, the dog crawling to get the ball, and the blood on the boy's hands.

The sensible, logical thing to do was to return the cart, pick up my horse, and head out. I'd killed two more of Powers's followers. That wouldn't please him at all. I'd probably need eyes in the back of my head to survive the day. But the fire was turning into a conflagration.

I wanted a bit more speed from the ol' plug pulling the cart, but didn't dare ask for it. As it was, she was huffing when we reached the livery. The owner, with whom I'd talked horses a few times in my meanderings about Gila Bend, began to saunter over to me to say hello, but when he saw the look on my face, he stopped and watched as I took a wind around the hitching rail with the reins and began a fast, stiff legged walk to the hotel. I noticed that the two corpses were gone, but their blood and blood of the dog was seeping slowly into the dirt.

This is none of my business. I'm being crazy. All I need to do is to ride away and it'll all be over. I'm setting myself up to be killed. This is plumb, stupid, goddamned insane.

The fire, however, was speaking much louder and much more urgently than my mind.

The judge had a room on the second floor of the hotel, although I didn't know which room it was. I climbed the stairs two at a time and started down the corridor, kicking each door solid and yelling, "Judge!"

His door opened before I got to it, and I saw the glint of metal of his Derringer as he stood in the doorway. He motioned me inside.

He had a table from the restaurant squeezed into his tiny room, and it was covered with papers, posters, and miscellaneous writs and so forth. The judge stood in front of the table.

"I want to do it," I said. "Where's that goddamn thing I'm supposed to sign? And I'm going to need money to fix the sheriff's office."

"Are you certain you've given this adequate thought?" the judge asked. "You seem . . . overwrought."

"Do you want me or not?"

"Yes—yes I do." He took the paper out of his coat pocket and a duplicate of it from his briefcase. "Sign both of these," he said, "down at the bottom where the line is."

I did so, the nib of the pen grinding into the paper from the excess force I was using to write.

"There's an oath I need to administer and then we'll . . ."

"C'mon, dammit, let's get this over with." I didn't pay much attention to the words I mumbled after the judge said them.

"Keep the document with you at all times, Mr. Taylor."

I refolded it and stuck it in my back pocket. I opened the door to leave. "Mr. Taylor, one more thing." He reached into his briefcase, fumbled around a bit and tossed something to me. I grabbed it out of the air and turned it flat on my palm. It was a silver star with the word *Sheriff* inscribed on it. I stepped out into the corridor and looked at that star in my hand for a long moment. Then I pinned it to my vest.

"Lord, what the hell am I doing?" I said aloud. I walked down the stairs considerably slower than I'd run up them. I needed a drink.

I stood at the bar. When I'd first pushed through the batwings all eyes turned on me. Obviously, the story about the two outlaws I'd gunned had gotten around quickly. The bartender drew me a beer without being asked. I asked him for a shot, too, and he reached for a bottle of swill in front of the mirror. "No," I said. "The drinkable stuff—not that hog-piss."

"But I can't—that's Billy's."

"That shit is all finished right now," I said. "You start serving up a decent drink no matter who asks for it."

"Is . . . is that badge for real?"

"You bet your ass it's real."

An outlaw moved from a table to stand next to me. "You ain't serious about sheriffin' in Gila Bend, are you?" he asked. "You already got enough trouble gunnin' those two boys today over a goddamn dog. That badge is gonna buy you a coffin real fast." He looked at the bartender. "Give him a drink," he said.

The 'tender poured a shot. The outlaw turned away.

"Wait," I said.

He turned back around.

"You haven't paid for the drink you just ordered for me," I said.

His face changed rapidly from incredulity to anger. I pushed my coat behind the grips of my Colt, making the move obvious.

The outlaw moved closer, close enough that his rotted teeth and whiskey breath made my gorge surge in the back of my throat.

"I ain't gonna draw on you," he said. "Ain't no sense in tusslin' over a drink, is there?"

His voice was nicely controlled, but his eyes conveyed a distinctly different message.

I was ready for his sucker punch. I stepped aside easily, and when his fist and forearm crossed the edge of the bar, I grabbed his wrist with my left hand and his arm—just before his elbow—

with my right. The combination of his weight and momentum helped me in the downward force I was exerting. The long bone between his wrist and his elbow snapped like a piece of dry kindling. He went to his knees, screeching in pain. I kicked him in the mouth, helping rid him of at least three or four of his diseased teeth. He fell to his side, semiconscious, moaning.

The four or five of Powers's followers who'd been at tables playing cards stood, glaring at me, but I didn't see much of a threat in their postures or their eyes. It's strange how that works: if they came at me, I had the order in which I'd shoot them flit into my mind—the short guy first, the man next to him, the fat slob at the table to the left, and so on. I put a dollar on the bar and said loud enough for everyone in the joint to hear.

"Fun time ends today, right now, for you trash. You either follow the law or you pay for the consequences. I'm a total, real, genuine goddamn sheriff now, and I'll kick some ass before I'm done."

There was some growling and mumbling but nothing that bothered me. "Tell Powers I'm at the hotel and I want to talk with him."

I downed the shot on the bar in front of me. After all, I'd paid for it. I could taste Kentucky woods in it, as well as the smoke of a hickory and mesquite fire. I was getting to like this fine booze no little bit.

"Where'd you get this whiskey?" I asked the 'tender.

"A local fella an' his brother make it," he said.

"They don't make a whole lot, but what they do produce is fine sippin' whiskey."

"It sure is," I agreed.

I went to my hotel room shoved the bed out of the direct line of fire through the door. The cheap wood wouldn't even slow down a .45 slug, much less stop it. I sat on the bed, leaning back against the headboard, awaiting company. I didn't have long to wait. I'd barely lit a cheroot when there were three heavy, measured thuds at the door.

"It's open," I called, pistol in my hand resting in my lap.

It wasn't Powers. It was, instead, one of the largest men I'd ever seen in my life. He was tall, but his size went well beyond height. His shoulders were hugely broad, and he'd ripped the sleeves off his shirt, apparently because the fabric couldn't restrain the bulging, flint-hard muscles of his arms and forearms. Even his denim pants were stressed by the muscles in his legs. He wore a gunbelt with a Smith & Wesson long-barreled .38 in it, but he wore it like an amateur—the holster high and resting too far toward his back for him to draw smoothly or rapidly. His face was placid, like those of so many men who know their own strength and don't need or care to exhibit it to anyone. He was beardless with good features: high cheekbones, a straight nose, a mouth that looked like it smiled often.

"You Pound?" he asked. His voice was deep and resonant, although he was young—somewhere between twenty and twenty-five I guessed.

"Yeah," I said. "I'm Pound."

"I hear tell you might be in need of a deputy—somebody to cover your back."

I hadn't really given any thought to hiring a deputy—maybe because I didn't think there was anyone in town who could be trusted. "I might be," I said. "Who're you?"

"My name is Don Murfin. I'm an uncle to Evan, the boy you helped bury his dog. Evan, he said you killed a couple of Powers's men for shootin' that poor dog. Me an' my family respect stuff like that."

"They needed killing," I said.

"For sure they did. It made good sense to me to come on into town and be your deputy."

I started to answer, but Don held up his massive hand to stop me.

"Look," he said, "lots of people figure 'cause I'm big, I'm stupid. That ain't true, Pound. Me an' my family, we make up a little whiskey from time to time. Some folks thought I'd be easy nuff to track down an' kill us an' then take over the whiskey trade. There must be a half dozen or more bodies buried up around our still."

"I wasn't about to say you were stupid, Don. What I was going to say is that there's a pretty good probability you'll end up dead. Powers is a sneaky sumbitch, and he has nothing at all against backshooting."

"I never planned to live forever, nohow. And us Murfins, we're a tight bunch. What you done for Evan you done for the whole slew of us. We pay our debts, and we figure we owe you. I got no wife or kids or nothin', so I'm the best one to help you out. An' if I get dropped, why there'll be another Murfin standin' beside you 'fore my corpse is cold."

I thought for a moment, then stood and extended my hand. Don Murfin took it and we shook, formally, as if sealing a business deal.

"I'll get you a star as soon as I can," I said. "The pay is that I'll buy you a beer every so often."

"Not two beers?"

I hesitated. "You drive a hard bargain, Don. But OK, two beers."

"Now," I said, "I think the first thing we need to do is to rebuild our office and the jail. The judge said he'd make sure everything is covered in terms of payment for a carpenter and whoever else we need. We need some . . ."

A loud rapping on the door interrupted me. I picked up my pistol from the bed and said, "It's open."

Powers walked in and closed the door behind him. His eyes were red—from anger or from booze, I couldn't tell. He glanced at Don and then focused on me.

"You killed two of my boys today," he said. "For shootin' a goddamn worthless dog that was worryin' their horses."

"The dog was nowhere near worthless, Powers," I said. "But you're right. I dusted two of your flunkies." I paused for a moment. "I kinda wish there'd been three or four of them, but a man has to play the cards dealt to him, no?"

"I'm awful tired of this shit, Pound. *Awful* tired. I see that judge made you a sheriff. That don't mean a goddamn thing to me. I'd as soon use that star as a target as not."

"I have a deputy, too," I said. "But he doesn't have a star yet," I said, and laughed a bit.

"I'm gonna tell you . . ."

"What you're going to do is listen, Powers," I snarled. "Don and me are going to clean up Gila Bend. There's no more free rides for you and your crew, no collections from the saloon owners, no gunfights in the street, no horse racing in the street. I hear your gamblers are crooked. Get rid of them. I hear you mistreat the whores and don't pay them 'cept with nickels and dimes. That'll stop. Lemme make this clear: starting right now, you people pay for what you drink or take out of the mercantile, you cut out the gunfights, and you pay your girls what they're worth. Anything else I think of, I'll let you know about."

Powers shook his head in amazement. "You're purely crazy," he said. "An' you won't leave Gila Bend alive. That's a promise on the heart of Robert E. Lee."

"The war's over, Powers," Don said. "Whether or not you and your crew believe it, it's true. This town is under the jurisdiction of the United States of America and all the country's laws apply right here as much as they do in Washington."

Powers's face turned yet more scarlet so that he looked apoplectic. "You're dead, too," he growled at Don.

Don moved a lot faster than one would think a man of his size could move. He grabbed Powers by the back of the neck and seat of his pants and threw him through the door. The door, of course, was closed.

Powers gathered himself up and got shakily to his feet. "The war ain't near over yet," he said, "'least between you two an' me." He limped down the corridor to the stairway. I wondered for a moment why he didn't draw, and then something became clear to me: he was a coward—afraid to face me or Don one-to-one. He needed the scum he rode with to give him courage. That was a good piece of information to have, and I wouldn't forget it.

Don and I briefed the judge before he left town. He gave us promissory notes that he said were as good as cash for whatever we needed to rebuild the office and jail and to buy whatever supplies we needed. He had another badge in his briefcase. It said *Sheriff* just like mine, but we didn't let that bother us.

The hammers of the carpenter and his helpers—friends of Don—rang several hours each day. Charred and broken wood was dragged out and replaced with new. We bought a rolltop at the mercantile but had to make the purchase and move the desk late at night because the mercantile owner was afraid of repercussions from Powers—but he was more afraid of losing the price he gouged out of the government for the desk.

I requisitioned far more substantial doors both at the street entrance and in the area leading from the office to the cells, figuring if Don and I came under siege, we wanted something substantial between us and our attackers. We bought six Remington .30-30s and a thousand rounds of good ammunition—not the army stuff. The carpenter built a rifle closet and Don and I each had a key.

I had a little innovation I asked the carpenter to make and install. I wanted a pull-down ladder that'd lead to the roof. Although the office was but a single story high, the perspective on the length of the street was better.

There was a bizarre lack of sound in Gila Bend, other than the working of the carpenter. The mercantile opened each day, but from my vantage point in front of the hotel, I saw that there was no traffic into the store—no citizens and no outlaws. The tension in the air was thick enough to swim in. Everyone knew something was going to happen, that Powers wouldn't relinquish his iron grasp on the town without a fight.

"Kinda like the lull before a storm," Don commented.

"Yeah. It is. Thing is, we have no idea which way the storm would hit us from."

That afternoon we carried our gear to the new office. We each slept in one cell, and we switched off watches so that only one of us slept at time.

After we started collecting prisoners, we'd have to make different arrangements.

The first skirmish came late one night. Don was on watch, and he called me to the front of the office. The bars were still open, but very few horses were tied at the rails. I pulled on my shirt and went forward to the office. Don pointed down the street toward the livery stable. Five or six torches burned orangish red in a cluster of riders.

"How about we try out them rifles?" Don asked. "Pick off a couple of 'em right where they are 'fore they charge us."

"Not yet," I said. We got out the rifles, loaded them, and each of us took three. The fresh, clean scent of gun oil clung to each weapon. "Prolly should've sighted these in before now," Don said. To that, he added, " 'Course it's kinda hard to miss an outlaw carryin' a torch comin' at us."

"How about I go up on the roof and you fight through the window and door down here?" I said. "Seems like that would give us the best coverage. Don't fire before I do—but take the sonsabitches down when you do. We don't want to burn out our nice new office."

I went up the ladder and pushed open the hatch. There wasn't much pitch to the roof; it was easy enough to sit or stand without fear of toppling. I arranged two of the .30-30s next to me and cradled the other in my arms.

I could hear the voices of the group fairly well. There was a whole lot of talk about "burnin' them shitheels out," and every so often the light from a torch would glint on a bottle being passed around.

The cluster broke into a jagged line. From the roof, I could see two of the horsemen with torches swing to the back of the buildings, apparently with a plan to get us from the rear.

If a person has ever heard a rebel yell, the sound of it will never be forgotten. It's more like the ululating moan-growl of some unearthly beast than of a human voice. The raggedy-assed and disorganized line started down the street howling the reb yell, holding their torches high, spurring their horses.

Don said something from downstairs that I missed.

"What?" I called to him. "What'd you say?"

He laughed. "Clever how they're sneaking up on us," he said.

I watched the two who were coming up from behind. I levered a bullet into the chamber of one of my .30-30s and set myself up in a nice position to blow the two outlaws to hell. I let them get real close before I fired. Don had been right about sighting in the rifles; my first shot ripped the horn off my target's saddle.

"Well, hell," I grunted in disgust, and aimed high and slightly to the left and fired again. The outlaw was plucked out of his saddle like kids make puppets jump around by pulling on the strings. The torch dropped to the dirt, flaring, illuminating the other rider quite clearly. Him I got with my first shot.

Downtairs, Don was cranking off rounds. I saw a horse go down in a mishmash of horse legs, a twisted human shape, and a blazing torch. The downed rider quickly caught fire.

Some slugs pinged on the roof around me, but nothing came too close. I picked up my second rifle and began firing at the few men stupid enough to keep riding hell-bent for leather toward our office. I picked one off easily. I heard the glass in our street window shatter and Don snarl, "Shit! That glass ain't cheap."

The remaining riders flung their torches futilely, the flames hitting the ground several yards from the office, and turned tail, hauling back down the street. I stayed on the roof for maybe another half hour peering up and down the street, looking for any action. The outlaw charge was so stupid, so poorly planned—if there was a real plan at all—that it was hard for me not to think that it was ruse of some kind. If it was a ploy, was it worth losing several men for? What did it accomplish?

The only thing I heard was a couple of shots from down toward the livery. Other than that, nothing was happening.

I came down the ladder, my face burning a bit from the blowback of the rifle. Don was still picking up shards of glass from in front of the window.

"What do you think?" I asked.

He shook his head as he dumped the broken glass into our wastepaper basket. "I dunno, Pound. I'd have to say that the whole damned thing smells fishy. No matter what else Powers is, he ain't stupid, an' that charge was just plain stupid."

"Yeah," I agreed. "I can't figure it, either. He has lots of men, but he can't throw them away like he did tonight."

Don went to the desk and took out a bottle of his whiskey and a two glasses. Without asking, he poured each glass four fingers full. I sat in the chair behind the desk with my feet up, lit a cheroot, and took a good swallow of the whiskey. "Damn," I said, "that's good stuff. I've had 'shine before and it was grain alcohol and whatever else the maker tossed in a pot. A fellow in Mexico told me that they'll throw a hog's head or a handful of snakes into the big pot to add flavor."

"Makin' pulque, no doubt. Shit. That stuff would strip the paint off a wall."

I got up and carried my glass to the window frame. It's a good thing I did. A single rider was approaching, riding hard, hunched over his saddle. I saw a quick flicker of light in whatever it was he was clutching. I grabbed a rifle and stepped out of the office. I had plenty of time to take a good bead and did so before I fired. I don't know where the hell the bullet went—but it didn't go where I aimed it.

Don handed me another rifle. "This here one is right, dead on," he said.

I took aim again. The rider was a lot closer— maybe fifty yards out. I fired and in the smallest part of a second I was thrown to my ass on the dirt by the concussion of the explosion of the dynamite the outlaw was carrying. The outlaw himself and his horse were blown to bits and shreds of flesh. For all I know, it might still be raining outlaw in some part of West Texas.

"Jesus," Don said, standing in the doorway. "Dynamite. I never gave it a thought."

"Me neither. We should have."

"I figure three sticks, maybe four," Don said. "One would be plenty to take us and our office out."

I finished my drink. "We're gonna need at least a couple of new men," I said. "We need to keep watch all the time—every minute—or we're dead. I'm not all that worried about an attack with rifles and pistols, but that dynamite scares the piss out of me."

"I can get a couple good men," Don said. "I got a pair of cousins, Jack and Joe, who live maybe a day out from here, raisin' some longhorns. Maybe they'll come."

"This isn't their fight . . ."

"Don't matter. They're family. I'll ride out soon's there's enough light."

It made sense. With two more men who could cover the office all the time from the roof and downstairs, Don and I would be freed up to make some changes in the town of Gila Bend. Don's "They're family," gave me a strange feeling. I had no one in the world I could call on for any kind of help, much less put their lives on the line.

"I guess you better get some sleep, then. I'll wake you as soon as there's a glimmer in the east."

Don took the rifle I'd used to blow up the outlaw and the horse. "This baby's goin' with me," he said. "An' let's bring the other ones outside town to true them up 'fore we need them again. Hell, one of 'em I used last night I couldn't hit a barn with if I was standin' five feet away from it."

Don left at very early daylight and the office seemed terribly empty as I sat there alone, with nothing in particular to do.

A sheriff who sits on his ass in his office isn't accomplishing anything. I ought to be out on the street— visible to both the honest citizens and the outlaws—and show them that the law had come to their town.

I hadn't gotten any real sleep, but I didn't feel at all tired. I was, however, hungry enough to eat a sack of horseshoes. I walked down to the hotel restaurant. I suppose it was something I need to get used to, but I felt the sights of a long gun lined up with my back with each step I took.

I took the back table where my back would be to the wall. That'd become a habit a long time ago, but I was getting a tad lax about it—like standing at the bar in the saloons. The girl who took my order—four eggs, a decent-sized sirloin, hashed potatoes, and plenty of coffee—looked around the place, saw that the other diners had no interest in what she was doing, and whispered, "Great job last night, Sheriff."

I ate every scrap on my plate and had four cups of coffee to wash the whole mess down.

I stopped at the mercantile, and the owner found he could spare me a box of thirty of those cheroots I'd gotten fond of. When I handed over the dollar fifty, he tried to refuse to take my money. "It doesn't work that way anymore," I said. "Anything that goes out of here is paid for first or put on an account by you. If one of Powers's men or anyone else tries to walk out without paying you let 'em go, but send a stockboy over to my office to fetch me or my deputy. OK?"

The storekeeper's smile was as broad as the desert horizon. "Yessir," he said. "I'll sure go ahead an' do that, Sheriff. Been too long that we . . ." The bell over the door rang and he cut off his sentence. That was fine; I knew what he was going to say.

I'd barely sat down behind my desk and was in the process of lighting up a cheroot when the door opened and Billy Powers strode in. I looked beyond him. It appeared that he was alone.

"I heard you had some trouble last night, Pound," he said.

I blew a very nicely formed smoke ring. "No, I can't say that we did. A little noisy late in the night, but that's about it. Just some drunken miners and cowpokes showin' their stupidity, is all. It was easy enough to quiet them down."

A flush of anger showed on Powers' face but his voice remained calm, almost affable. "You know you're fightin' a loser battle here, don't you?"

"No," I smiled, "I don't know that at all."

"There's plenty of pie to cut up here, Pound— enough for all of us."

"Out," I said.

Powers looked perplexed.

"Get out of my office—do it now or I'll pick you up and throw you out."

Powers forced a grin. "You're mine," he said. "No matter what else happens, you're mine."

"I wouldn't have it any other way."

He stomped out of the office, slamming the door behind him.

Time, once again, began to drag. There were almost no street sounds and only a few horses tied in front of the various gin mills. My eyes fell on the rifle closet and the five weapons in it. I grinned. Sighting them in would be a job I'd enjoy and one that needed doing. I filled my front pockets with cartridges and wrapped the rifles in my blanket from the cell I'd been sleeping in.

I'd almost walked by the apothecary without seeing it. It was in the front of what looked like a warehouse or storage facility of some kind. The only thing that indicated the business was a brass plaque with the word APOTHECARY. Out of curiosity, I walked in. All the standard patent medicines, potions, and elixirs were placed neatly—almost precisely—on shelves behind the glass-fronted counter. On the counter itself was a ledger, and a mortar and pestle. Behind the glass were several different types of trusses and supports.

The elderly lady who came out from the back of the building was the perfect grandmother: slightly chubby, a cherubic face and a wide smile, wearing a pristinely white apron over her dress. "Help you?" she asked.

"No, ma'am. I'm just looking right now, but I'll sure keep your store in mind should the need arise."

"Why, thank you, son," she said.

I felt guilty for not buying anything.

As I approached the stable, the owner came rushing out to meet me. "Mr. Pound," he said, "I'm terrible awful sorry. There was nothin' I could do. I . . ."

I shifted the wrapped rifles to my left shoulder, freeing up my right if I needed to pull my Colt. "What's the matter? What happened?"

"Well, see—it's your horse . . ."

I pushed by the old guy and rushed to the stall where my horse had been kept when he wasn't out in the pasture. He was dead, crumpled in a clumsy position on the straw bedding. There were two bullet holes in his head.

Chapter Four

I stood there at the stall staring at my horse. The metallic-sweet scent of blood was strong and cloying in the close air of the barn. He was positioned more or less on his left side, but any horseman knows that when a horse is down and dead the rigor mortis tugs their legs into positions they'd never take in life. There's a lot of blood in a horse—mine must have been killed several hours ago—yet there were tiny streams of blood still seeping from his head.

He'd been a hell of a horse—there seemed to be no bottom to him, nothing he wouldn't do if I asked him to do it. "Heart," horse people call it. This boy had more heart than any horse I've ever owned or come across in the course of my life.

I called the stableman over. "Here's what I want," I said. "I want a hole dug out in the prairie at least five or six feet deep—no less. It needs to be wide enough to take this horse. I'll check on this. You don't want me to find my orders haven't been followed."

"Well, yessir," the liveryman said, "I can do that, but it's going to cost you. I'd say maybe . . ."

I handed him a fifty-dollar bill. "Just get it done. Go out and hire some diggers right now. Enough men can heft him onto a farm wagon. If this horse is here after dark, you're going to regret it."

He hustled off, leaving me with my horse.

That fire in me had been banked and tempered a bit. Just now it erupted, flaring and burning as strongly as it ever had, so that I could barely contain it. My palms were sweating so much the grips of my Colt were wet. I hadn't realized I'd reached for my .45, but I obviously had.

I walked away from my good horse for the last time. There was a throwin' rope hanging on a peg and I took it as I walked to the door that led to the pasture. The lariat felt good in my hands, although I hadn't worked beef in a good long time.

I went out to the pasture. Most of the horses the stable owner had were remounts for the army cavalry—which meant, almost by definition, that they were either doped-up mustangs, had really bad habits such as chewing on riders, or were docile plugs that were presented to be seven or eight years old but in truth were closer to twenty.

There were, however, a few good animals in the small herd. I dropped a loop over a muscular black stud and looked him over. I liked him. But there were a couple of things wrong. His pasterns had no slope to them—he'd be like riding in a buckboard with square wheels. And he was a tad jittery. Still, he was a pretty good horse—just not the one for me.

I roped a pretty mare and found that she was skittish and more than a little crazy. When I followed down my rope to her, she swung her ass around, dropped her head, and kicked out with both rear hooves; either hoof connecting with a man's head would have killed him.

I dropped a loop over a nice buckskin's neck. The rope didn't seem to bother him at all. He was well-built: lots of chest, good withers and back, and good, broad, strong hindquarters. He'd lost his eggs to a gelding knife a long time ago. That didn't bother me; I had nothing at all against a good gelding. On the spot, I decided to buy him. If I had riding, reining, or control problems, I figured I could bring him into line. He had that look of intelligence in his deep chestnut eyes. I turned him loose and went to talk with the stable owner, who was loading pickaxes and shovels onto a small wagon.

"What do you need for that buckskin?" I asked.

"Oh, him," the old fellow said. "He's a pure goddamn jewel, is what he is. Why, he . . ."

"Cut the shit," I said. "How much?"

"I gotta get eighty dollars for that horse—not a penny less."

"Your ass." I counted out sixty-five dollars and handed over the cash.

"Sold," the ol' guy said.

"I want new shoes on him all the way around

before I come back a little later. I'll pay the blacksmith. And tell him to leave plenty of frog. I could be riding through some rough country."

The stableman grinned. "Damned if you don't know your horses, son," he said. "That tissue on the underside of the hoof is right important in keeping a horse from laming up. I'll have a kid fetch the smith right off."

The fire inside me was still blazing as I fetched the buckskin into a stall and fit my saddle on his back and cinched him up. He stood well, without drawing in air to make his gut expand like some horses will do. He took my low port cutting horse bit easily.

I searched the bottom of my saddlebag and found what I was after: a cylinder of solid steel about four inches long and an inch in diameter with slight indentations in it so that it fit my clenched right fist perfectly. I plucked a crab apple from a basket of them the livery kept around as training rewards and walked out of the barn.

The heat was already strong enough to make my neck sweat. I ignored it. I walked toward my hotel with that lump of cold steel in my hand.

Sometimes things work out as they should, and this situation did just that. Three men from Powers's crew rode up from behind me and jigged their horses to match my stride. They were already drunk or close to it, but not falling out of their saddles—just all mouth, laughing too much and too loud.

"Hey, Sheriff," one said, "how come you're

walkin'? That busted down ol' plug of yours finally croak?"

"Shit," another said, "that there horse was three-quarters dead when this silly sumbitch rode him into town."

"You'd best have the carcass dragged way the hell outta Gila Bend," the third said, "'fore he gits to rottin' good an' stinks up the whole town—just like a lawman does."

I stopped walking, and the three outlaws reined in. I untied the latigo that tied my holster and pistol tight to my leg, then unbuckled my gunbelt.

"As you litter of pigs can see," I said, "I'm unarmed. I've got a couple hundred dollars and a bit more in my pocket. You cowards care to step down and settle things out with our fists—and get my cash, too?"

"An' our boots, too," an outlaw said. "Our fists an' our boots."

"Sure. Boots, too. That's fine with me."

The inferno was now burning too hot for me to even begin to control. While the three outlaws were joking among themselves about kicking my ass as they swung down from their horses, I grabbed the one closest to me and hit him in the face as hard as I could with my right fist. There was a crack of bone or cartilage or whatever. As he was going down, I kicked him square in the eggs.

The other two were moving fast at me. The first one made a dive-type tackle attempt, but I stepped aside easily and landed a truly powerful shot to the back of his neck. He went down and stayed down.

The third was the fighter of the group. He danced around me in classic boxing form, fists tight, protecting his face. He hit me with a left that I didn't even see coming, shaking me, opening a cut over my right eyebrow. I backed, but the outlaw stayed with me. A right split my lower lip, and another left widened and deepened the slash over my eye.

I kept my fists up to cover myself and backed again. The outlaw laughed and came on. I kicked him in the knee and then as he collapsed, I laid into his face with my right fist. My left was in there, too, but it wasn't doing near the damage my right and my lump of steel were doing. I purely took him apart. I worked his head like it was one of those punching-bag things. His nose splayed on his face, gushing blood, both his eyes were swollen and cut, and a few of his front teeth littered the dirt of the street. I hurt him bad, and that's what I wanted—needed—to do. My own knuckles were torn to hell and the cut over my eye still bleeding, but that was a small enough price to pay.

My personal fire receded.

I was in control again.

I was a little shaky, and my knuckles were bleeding. I'd taken a few good shots from the third outlaw, the cut over my eye was still pouring blood, and there was a buzzing-running water sound in my head. But I was OK. I'd been hurt a lot worse in my day. I picked up my gunbelt, tied my holster down, and set out to the livery to fetch my new horse.

There was an open tin of udder balm on a shelf in the barn, and I spread some across my knuckles and globbed some on the cut over my eye. That udder balm is good stuff—it stops bleeding better than anything else I know of.

I'd already tied my bundle of .30-30s where a bedroll would go on a working cowhand's saddle. I dropped my piece of steel back into my saddlebag and led the buckskin out of the barn and climbed aboard. The sun hit his coat and his golden copper coloring was a thing of beauty. I stepped into a stirrup and settled myself on the buckskin's back.

He had an easy mouth, which is certainly rare in Western ranch horses. A working cowpoke doesn't develop any more friendship with one of the horses in his string than a storekeeper does for an apron.

A slight tap at the reins stopped the horse perfectly and laying a rein lightly against either side of his neck eased him into a turn. I noticed he always kept under himself—ready to go in any direction.

I rode to the end of the street and out of the town, out to the prairie. I was raising dust, but this time no one seemed to be following me.

I gave the buckskin some rein and thumped my spurless heels on his side. He was in a full gallop in a couple of strides and he had the

Thoroughbred way of running: stretching his body to pull long pieces of ground under him. I couldn't see any signs of Thoroughbred blood in him, but I was more than sure there was some back there somewhere in his parentage.

I eased him back to a lope when sweat broke on his chest. I pulled my Colt and fired three times into the air. My horse flinched, of course, but didn't show any fear and held to his lope without missing a stride. I rubbed his neck and reined him down to a walk.

When I thought I was in a good place to work the rifles, I stopped and dismounted and tried the horse on ground tying. I eased the reins over his head so they touched the ground, said, "Stay," and walked away. He stood there like a marble statue.

Like I said, sometimes things work out good.

I picked a saguaro about fifty yards out as a target. I used a coin to adjust the sights because I'd forgotten to bring a small screwdriver along.

Three of the rifles I needed to do considerable screwing around with to bring them dead-on. One of the others was perfect as it was. The other took only a minor adjustment to true up.

Of course, the rifles would shoot a bit high at distances less than fifty yards, but it'd take only a single shot to tell Don or me that. Then we'd aim a frog hair lower and kick some ass.

I put my horse up in the livery—my dead animal was already gone—and took the rifles to the office and set them butt down in the gun closet. I didn't have much to do and considered a cold beer. I lit a cheroot as I pondered.

I guess it didn't take long for Billy Powers banged-up men to get back to him.

He bashed the door open, slamming it against the inside wall.

"You dirty sonofabitch," he bellowed, his face as red as Italian wine. "I've had just about enough of you screwing with me and my men. Those three you attacked are hurtin' pretty bad, and they're useless to me until they heal. You're pissin' me off real bad, Pound, and people who piss me off end up dead."

"Nice to see you too, Billy," I said. "Fine morning, isn't it? I'd like to offer you coffee, but the stove we ordered from Chicago hasn't come in yet. Damn shame, ain't it? We ordered that little stove some time ago."

Powers sputtered a bit before he could get his words out. "You think you're the top gun around here, Pound. You ain't. I am. Understand?"

I grinned at him. "Fine," I said. "Let's go out on the street right now and have a draw an' fire contest. The winner gets to stay alive."

"I ain't . . ."

"What you *ain't* is ready to face me without your flunkies set to blow me to pieces if it looks like I'm faster than you, right? 'Course you could always use that goddamn buffalo hunter who rides with you and uses a Sharps. He could drop me from a couple-three hundred yards out—in the back—before you and me ever faced off."

Powers face was apoplectic.

Don walked in and saw what was going on. "Billy," he said cheerfully, "good to see you. I sure hope you brought some coffee, 'cause the stove we ordered ain't come in yet from Chicago."

Powers glared at Don for a moment, then put his hand on the deputy's chest to move him from blocking the doorway. Insanely angry as Powers was, and how his face was scarlet and twisted, surprise still registered. Trying to push Don Murfin was like trying to push over a marble column.

"Lemme out," Powers demanded.

"Why sure," Don said. "Just as soon as you say . . ."

He started the word "please" when I said, "Don," and shook my head very slightly from side to side. Don stepped out of the way, and Billy Powers stormed out, mumbling to himself.

"You'll get your chance with Powers," I said. "But we can't face that army of his right now."

Don shrugged, then nodded. "OK." He tugged a coin from his pocket and flipped it into the air. "Heads, we go get a cup of coffee, tails we get a beer." He flipped the coin again and slapped it on his palm. "Heads," he said, "but I meant two out of three. I just didn't say it out loud, is all."

"Right," I said.

We got up to six out of ten before the coin relented and set us off to a saloon. We selected the one with the fewest horses hitched out front. We wanted to talk, and shouting over the racket of drunks isn't talking. We took our schooners of beer to a table and settled in.

"I heard about your little do-si-do this morning," Don said. "Sorry about your horse. He was a good one."

"Yeah. He was."

"The way I heard the story is that the two of us jumped the Powers boys swinging two-by-fours."

"That's exactly the way it happened," I said, "but if I recall, we were using clubs stouter than two-by-fours."

We laughed and drank some beer. "My cousin does some horse trading, Pound, and he 'most always has a few head that're worth owning. I can check . . ."

"I bought a real fine horse from the livery," I said.

Don smiled. "That buckskin, right? The rest of them looked like buzzard bait. That buckskin—what does he know?"

"A whole lot," I said proudly. "He reins perfectly, isn't afraid of gunfire, and I swear he's the fastest horse I ever rode."

"Damn," Don said appreciatively. "Where'd he come from?"

"Probably stolen. But there's no brand or other identifying mark on him. I got real good papers from the livery."

"I wonder if you shouldn't cut his lip to get an identifying scar, Pound, or maybe get a brand on him."

"I won't cut his lip, and I don't want a brand, either. My papers are good enough."

"Nutted?"

"Yeah. He's not interested in the mares."

"Sounds like a hell of a horse."

"You won't get an argument from me on that," I said.

Don went to the bar and brought back a couple more beers. "I was thinkin'," he said, "I'd take a ride on home an' see how many boys I can get together an' ready to fight in a hurry."

"Good idea."

He took a long swallow of beer. "I'm kinda wonderin' what's going to keep Powers's men from shooting your buckskin like they gunned your bay."

"I thought about that. I'm going to post a watch-man at the stable every night."

"Who you gonna get?"

"I was thinking Calvin, the drunk. I figure if I give him a bottle every morning he'd by fairly sober by night."

"Jesus, Pound—that ol' bar-rag is useless."

"Maybe. We'll see."

"Look, Pound, I've got a better idea than using that rum-dumb at all for anything. I got a fella who up an' married my sister—done the right thing by her. Thing is, I hadda chase the sumbitch halfway 'cross Texas. Anyway, he's a handy type and a good carpenter. Why don't I bring him on back with me an' we'll have him build a shelter right out behind the cells? I ain't talkin' about a barn—jus' a three-sided shelter to keep our animals outta the rain and wind—an' maybe a bit of hay storage room, too. An' as to fightin', he'd take on Goliath outta the Bible and purely kick his ass."

"That sounds real good, Don. What's the fellow's name?"

"Lucas is what he goes by. I'll ask you not to go through them Wanted posters too close—he's got some money on his head."

"No problem there. You'll be back tonight?"

"Most likely—tomorra morning at the latest. Lucas has a little wagon he hauls behind a donkey with his tools an' such in it. Might take him a bit longer, but he'll get here."

Don wasn't one to put things off; he left our office, collected his horse from the livery, and went off on his way home.

It's odd: I didn't know whether Don had a honey he missed and who missed him. Because a man isn't married doesn't mean he doesn't have a lover.

A pair of horses galloped by the office, and I barely caught them with my edge of my eye through our small window. The riders were leaning over their horse's withers, and the animals were running their hearts out. I couldn't see who was ahead, so I went to the window. The horses seemed perfectly matched. I stood there, wanting to see who took the race.

These two boys couldn't have been among Powers's crew—neither wore a gunbelt, and when they reined in they laughed and did some back-slapping and shook hands. They rode back into town, no doubt headed for a saloon.

'Course, early on I'd said there'd be no horse racing in Gila Bend. But hell, these two boys, probably silver mine workers or cowpokes from the looks of them, weren't causing any problems or trouble. They were simply cutting loose, with maybe a couple of weeks of wages in their pockets, just itching and twisting to be spent.

I sat back down, put my heels up on the desk, and just let my mind drift.

I'd never planned to teach school. I wanted to be a writer—but not that sensational bullshit that'd become so popular in the East. I wanted to write novels that reached deep into the human condition. I wanted my characters to be *real* people—not stereotyped puppets. It didn't work out quite that way. I fell in love with booze and didn't let it go for about fifteen years, until I met met Zeb Stone.

I liked women well enough, but they didn't seem to take to a falling down, gaping-mouthed loser who pissed his pants fairly frequently when he passed out on the floor of a saloon.

When I got semistraight with Zeb and we started robbing and killing folks, there wasn't any time for ladies. Once in a while, though, depending on where Zeb and I were, I'd get my ashes hauled.

It wasn't good, but I suppose it was better than nothing.

Or maybe not.

The concept of being married appealed to me—marriage and a family seemed like a divinely peaceful way to live out a life, not at all what my own family was like.

At times, when I think of families, I get to feeling a little envious. Don and his relatives all living in close proximity to one another must have been nice.

My old man didn't say a dozen words a day—none of them to me unless he was bitching that I didn't work hard enough or long enough. Jesus. An army of sodbusters couldn't coax a decent crop out of the sand and rocks that comprised Pa's sixty acres.

My ma reminded me—and still does—of a sheep: large, clumsy, hairy, and plain stupid. She'd have to be stupid to stay with my father. He hit her every so often, and she accepted that as part of the marriage contract, I guess.

Both of them sweated all summer and froze their asses off every winter. I couldn't figure it out. Had I been either of them, I'd have climbed onto one of the busted-down plow horses and gone somewhere—anywhere.

It could be that the hardscrabble life is what made me take to bank robbing so readily, or to the bottle before I became a criminal. I'd far rather catch a few slugs from the law and go out that way than work myself to death in the sun, cursing everyone and everything because I had such a lousy life and couldn't get a break.

* * *

Don and Lucas arrived late that night, both drunk. They didn't make a bit more noise than would a herd of buffalo stampeding through the office. I heard them carry some things inside—Lucas's tools, probably. They finally settled down or passed out—whichever, didn't matter to me as long as they kept quiet. Don slept in his usual cell and Lucas on the floor next to the desk in the front part of the office. Don grabbed my sleeve as I was checking that he wouldn't suffocate himself.

"Pound," he said drunkenly, "you're outta luck in bringin' more of our family. It ain't that they can't fight, but my pa said this ain't his fight and to screw the whole buncha us. So that's it—no more family fightin' here. An Pa—he don't change his mind."

The neighborhood roosters woke me up, just as they did every morning. I pulled on my boots—I slept in my shirt and pants because I didn't know when I'd be called out by the good citizens of Gila Bend. I took a look at Don. He looked and smelled dead: mouth hanging open, vomit down the front of his shirt, one boot on and the other tossed into the corner of the cell. I knew he was alive, though. His phlegmy snorting and snoring established that.

Lucas was stretched out next to the desk, sleeping peacefully. His gunbelt was draped over the desk chair. It was of good leather, very nicely tooled. A piece of latigo hung down from the bottom of the holster. The holster itself was empty.

Lucas was using a saddle blanket for a kind of pillow and his right hand was tucked under the blanket next to his head. I didn't have to be a genius to figure out where his pistol was, and I was more than a little concerned about waking him, surprising him. While I was pondering how I could make my presence known without getting shot, Lucas's eyes popped open. They were a very dark and piercing blue, and there was not even a hint of drunken redness or morning-after crud in the corners.

"You Pound?" he asked. His voice was deep, resonant, pleasant enough to the ear with none of the raspiness that follows a night of boozing.

"You might better learn not to sneak up on a sleeping man," he said. He pulled his right hand out from under the saddle blanket, holding a Colt .45 with the front and rear sights filed away.

"See why?" he said.

"Well, I'll tell you, Lucas: I could have gunned you as you slept with no trouble at all."

"There's that, 'course," he said. "You got any coffee?"

"Nothing to heat it on. But come on—the hotel down the street has a little restaurant."

Lucas's face lit up. "Restaurant? Hot damn! I'm purely starved to death."

I got a good look at Lucas when he stood and strapped on his gunbelt. He was cut from the same mold as Don: tall, broad shouldered, with a narrow waist. The man exuded strength. For whatever reason he put me in mind of a mountain cat ready to spring. His face was planes and angles and his hair—little-girl blond in color—far below his shoulders. I noticed that the thumb of his left hand was missing, and he caught me gawking.

"A bounty hunter in Laredo was faster'n me, but he was a lousy shot. I didn't need my left thumb to kill the sumbitch. I hardly miss the thumb; anyways, that was a good long time ago." Then he added, "I'm a lot faster now than I was then. And I shoot real good."

I nodded but had nothing to add. "I'm thinking," I said, "I might try to wake Don up to come along, but I suppose that's a lost cause."

"Yeah, it is. Plus, he stinks."

We walked to the hotel without much to say, Lucas looking around at the stores and bars. I ordered four eggs, lots of bacon, hash-brown potatoes, and a pot of coffee. Lucas asked for the biggest beefsteak they had in the place, a dozen fried eggs, fried potatoes, and another pot of coffee.

"I already ordered up a pot, Lucas," I said.

"Yeah, but you never seen me drink coffee. I still amaze my ma-in-law an' the rest of the family."

The waitress brought the coffee first. Lucas attacked his as if it were an ice cold beer after a long, hot day of following a plow horse's ass.

"I hear you done banks, you an' your pard," Lucas said, refilling his cup.

"Yeah. We did one stagecoach, too, but that didn't work out well, so we stuck with banks. I did one stage by myself—an army pay wagon."

"Good hit?"

"You bet."

"Now me," Lucas said, "I was always partial to coaches, an' I done good with them. Hell, all you gotta do is take out the shotgun rider an' you're all set. Most all the drivers ain't concerned about their passengers' money, or money they was carrying for anybody else. They preferred to stay alive. I rode with Butch and Sundance for a while, but they was crazy. Anyway, I like working alone."

"What's the paper out on you for?" I asked.

"Murder, robbery, rape, escape from federal authorities, all that shit. Hey, let me ask you somethin'. You got some kinda deal for bein' sheriff here for a year. If you live it out, you get a pardon, no?"

"Yeah, that's right."

"What about me? If I joined up, would I get one of them pardons, too?"

"I dunno. I'll look into it, Lucas."

We ate for a while in silence, enjoying our food. Finally, I said, "You married Don's sister, right?"

"Had to. She was up the stump, and Don tracked me down. Rose of Sharon is her name. The baby was a girl, jus' as goddamn cute as a young bunny."

He chewed and swallowed a large chunk of steak and then said, "See, my ma-in-law—hell, I just call her ma—she takes care of my kid. My wife, she run off with a guitar player." He shook his head. "At times I kinda miss her, but that boy could play the livin' piss outta a guitar. He played on a twelve string. You ever heard one?"

"I don't think . . ."

"He sometimes played darkie music, an' it was like nothin' you ever heard before. Used one of them sliders on his left hand to make that guitar talk. That music, well, it was raw like corn whiskey an' driving, ya know? I never heard no white music like that."

I ate more of my breakfast until Lucas talked again. He averted his eyes as he spoke.

"I'd bet my grannie's ass that fella had some darkie blood in him, maybe from way back. He was as white as you or me, but there was somethin' about the way he moved, and 'course how he played that twelve string."

I figured it was a good time to leave the subject behind. "If you can put together some kinda list of the materials you'll need to build the shelter and your time into it, I can get it off so it gets paid quick. I suggest you gouge the piss outta everything you need—it's government money."

"Sure. I can do that. Thing is, I was thinkin' of building the shelter with room for three horses, without them tusslin' or chewin' hide outta each other."

"But, Lucas," I said, "it's just me and Don. We really don't need . . ."

Lucas cut me off. "I was thinkin' maybe I'd join on with you boys. I'm weary of makin' whiskey an' settin' on Ma an' Pa's porch. I'm a man who likes some action, and I'd get that here. Right?"

I couldn't answer his offer quickly enough. "I'll order up a badge and get you on the payroll, although the money doesn't amount to a bedbug's fart in a hurricane. I'm real glad to have you, Lucas, real glad. And I'll look into that pardon."

We shook hands and the deal was set and sealed.

Lucas started the project out back by erecting a good post and rail fence so the horses could soak up sunshine whenever they cared to. Don was right about Lucas: he was a hell of a carpenter. He put up a three-sided shelter with a small loft for hay storage in a matter of a few days, and he ran a pipe from our well that fed into a trough so the animals would always have fresh water. The whole project was a fine piece of work, and we moved our horses into it, packed some hay in the loft, filled the trough, and stood back to watch the horses' reaction. Like I once said, a horse is damned near as smart as a sack of cow turds. The three of ours moved right into the enclosure and then stood around shagging flies with their tails. I suppose their new quarters could have been the gates to hell and they wouldn't have paid any particular attention.

We had to store our tack—saddles, bridles, blankets, reins, and the other miscellaneous things a horseman needs—just inside the rear door, a few feet from Don's cell. I thought maybe we should get a cot or something for Lucas to sleep on—after all, it was only government money. But he said he was perfectly comfortable sleeping on the floor in the front office, so I didn't push the matter.

So. It was the hottest part of August, and there was precious little difference between when the sun was exerting its power or when it was full dark. The incessant heat made good dogs—even some cattle dogs—either go after their masters or tear hell out of other dogs. It was that kind of heat. Horses did some bucking in the morning when they were first saddled up, but they weren't playing or screwing around: they wanted to get that rider off and maybe step on him. I'm not talking here about unbroken horses—I mean horses men had used and trusted for a long time. This goddamn heat would have made Jesus Howard Christ peevish: it sure did turn good men around.

I didn't pay much attention to fistfights in the gin mills unless the battle turned to guns. I figured it this way: let the dumb bastards settle their own disputes with their fists and boots.

The three of us sat around the office. Lucas had made a sign that hung over our door outside, saying SHARIFF. Not only was Lucas a fine carpenter, he could make and letter the very ass off a sign.

Lucas had done his sign work out by the enclosure, so neither I nor Don paid much attention to what he was doing. One morning he nailed it up and brought Don and me out to see it. Lucas had the proud and happy glint in his eyes of a school-kid bringing home an A to his folks.

I cleared my throat needlessly. "Well, Lucas," I said, "it's a beautiful sign—a perfect sign . . . except you spelled 'sheriff' wrong."

"Ahhh, shit," he said dejectedly.

"Probably ain't three people in Gila Bend who'd know the difference," Don said. "It's a real fine sign, Lucas."

Lucas backed up a couple of steps, keeping his eyes focused on the sign. "Ain't no use in doin' a job of work unless the sumbitch comes out right."

I'd seen men attempt to fan a .45. Most of them were slow and inept. Lucas wasn't. I was standing there looking at him and I barely saw his draw, it was so smooth and so fast. He fanned the hammer on his pistol so that the six reports sounded like one. His left hand—the fanning hand—didn't move more than a few inches. The boys I'd seen had made elongated, sweeping motions that looked clumsy and slow—both of which they were.

Bits, shards, and splinters seemed to jump from the sign. Lucas reloaded his pistol and dropped it back into his holster.

"Well, anyways," he said, "it's good I bought some extra paint an' had some planks left over," he said. "But Jesus Howard Christ on a bronc, what the hell difference does spelling make? Shit."

I considered it wise not to launch into a lecture on the importance of proper spelling in the English language.

The three of us went back into the office. Lucas sat on the edge of the desk, his boot tapping on the floor in a frenetic nonrhythm. Don was reading a dime Western with the title across the front cover, *Saving Sweet Sally—Dan'l Boone Enters the Fray!* Underneath the title was, *A True Adventure*.

I'd looked at the magazine earlier but had to give it up when ol' Dan'l put slugs directly down the barrels of the guns of the miscreants who'd captured Sweet Sue.

I pushed some papers around, none of which meant much of anything. I'd written to the judge about putting Lucus on as a deputy and about a pardon for him with the same stipulation mine carried.

Our postmaster opened the door, tossed my mail on my desk, and left. She wasn't what you'd call affable.

There was a letter from the judge. I opened it and read:

> . . . *job was given to you along with great and highly beneficial benefits. However, bringing a mindless, bloodthirsty cutthroat such as Mr. Lucas Chambery would have no ameliorative function. Your request and petition here is hereby denied* . . .

I didn't see any good reason not to tell Lucas about the judge's refusal right then and there: holding on to bad news doesn't do anyone any good.

I handed the letter to Lucas.

His face reddened. "I don't read real good," he said.

I took the letter back and read its contents to him. His face didn't change—I suppose neither one of us had anticipated a favorable response. Still, it was a disappointment. Lucas's expression didn't change at all, nor did the tapping of his boot, which, quite frankly, was driving me crazy.

After a while he said, "The way I see, it's a matter of bein' in the right place at the right time. If I'd been in Gila Bend, I might could've been the one the judge offered the pardon to."

"I hope there are no hard feelings," I said.

"Hard feelin's? Nah. Look, when I see a man who has somethin' I might wanna have, do I have hard feelings against him? Hell, no—'cept if it's money or a horse." He paused for a moment. "Or maybe a real fine woman," he added. A moment later, "Or a spread of land I cotton to. An' maybe a real good saddle."

I had the feeling that he could go on for quite some time with things he might resent others for having. "Well," I said. "Are you staying on, Lucas? If you want to head on home, that's fine. I don't know as I'd blame you."

"I ain't goin' nowhere," Lucas said. "It's like I told you a bit ago: I was gettin' right antsy with doin' nothin' but makin' whiskey, settin' on the front porch, an arguin' with Pa. I'm staying," he said, with a strong note of finality.

"One thing you could do for me is to stop tapping that goddamn boot on the floor. Jesus, it's irritating."

"Feisty today, ain't you?" He grinned. "Sure, I'll stop tappin' my boot. I didn't know it was grindin' on you boys."

Lucas shoved his butt back on the desk a bit. The silence was wonderful. Then he began tapping his right index finger on the wood.

"Ahh, shit," I said.

"Lucas, he's always been like that," Don explained. "Always tappin' or fidgeting or hummin' or some damned thing. He don't mean nothin' by it."

"Look," I said, "I'd be pleased to buy you boys a beer. How's that sound?"

Both men were on their feet before my words faded.

"I jus' might take you up on that." Lucas smiled.

"Me too," Don said. "I'm damned near thirsty enough to drink sand and enjoy the hell outta it."

We left the office and headed down the street, walking three abreast. I remember seeing a picture of Wyatt, Doc, and Morgan walking just like the three of us were, down the street in Dodge, I think it was. I admit I kinda liked the image.

There were a half dozen horses tied in front of the joint that served the coldest beer, and that's where we headed.

The reek inside the place was, as usual, composed of sweat, stale beer, and tobacco smoke. We stood inside the batwings letting our eyes adjust to the murkiness. There were four card tables in Us and a half dozen or so fellows standing at the bar.

Conversation stopped the moment we entered. The men at the bar moved back to the tables, carrying their beer and shot glasses.

"Right lively in here," Lucas commented.

"We didn't come here to visit with this bunch of backshooters," I said.

"Let's drink us some beer," Don said. He waved to the bartender and held up three fingers. The 'tender looked at him and then looked away quickly.

I walked down the length of the bar to where he stood. "My deputy ordered up three beers," I said. "You'd best serve them up."

"I . . . I can't serve you no beer or whiskey," he said, his voice nervous and trembly. "If it was up to me, I would—but it ain't up to me."

"Powers tell you to shut the three of us off?"

"Yes . . . yessir, he did."

I went back to where Don and Lucas stood.

"The 'tender says Billy Powers told him not to serve us."

"No problem there," Lucas said. "I can pull a beer as good as any man."

He vaulted over the bar and took three mugs from the shelf under the bottles and began to fill them from the barrel spigot.

The men who'd been playing cards all stood.

"Dammit," I mumbled, "all I wanted was a beer."

Chapter Five

A spokesman, drunk enough to appoint himself as such, approached us at the bar.

"Hold on for a second," I said. "I have something real important to say—something that needs to be said before someone gets hurt."

"Backin' down, chickenshit?" the spokesman said. He smiled, showing a full collection of yellow-brown, crooked teeth. "Go 'head an' have your say," he said magnanimously, as if he were doing us a giant favor.

I cleared my throat and took a sip of my beer. I came away with a white foam mustache. "Deputy Lucas," I said, "you pull a truly piss-poor beer." I held my schooner up for all to see. "Lookit this goddamn thing—four inches of foam." I hurled the mug at the mirror behind the bar. The breaking of bottles and mirror glass was wonderful to hear.

"Pound, I hate to agree with you—or any goddamn body—against a relative," Don said, "but I gotta be with you on this one." He looked over at Lucas. "You're a failure, boy. Now do it again an' do her right."

"Yessir," Lucas said. He began to draw a beer but stopped.

"This here's the problem—not my pourin'. Sumbitch of a spigot screws up. I can fix her, though." He drew his .45 and put two bullets into the beer barrel, maybe an inch or so from the bottom. Beer spewed happily out of the jagged holes in the barrel.

The spokesman came at me, swing crazily, but connecting with nothing but fetid, smoke-filled air. I dropped him with a single punch—a long right-hand roundhouse. The spokesman went down to stay for several minutes. I was proud of that punch.

The others in the saloon charged, a couple of them brandishing chairs.

Lucas watched Don and I tussle with the outlaws, and he downed a beer from one of his bullet holes. Then he vaulted back over the bar and joined the fight.

There were a couple of strong, fighting men in Powers's group, and Lucas went right for them. He kicked the first one in the orbs, which was good for at least three days of pain for the outlaw.

The second tough came at Lucas in the Marquis de Queensbury stance and posture. Lucas grabbed up a chair and smashed it over the boxer's head, and he went down.

Look, I hadn't done much bar fighting in the course of my criminal career and none before that. It simply made no sense to me. Nevertheless, two of Powers's men were trading me off; first one would hit me and then the other. Neither one could throw much of a punch, but they were hurting me nevertheless.

When I was floored for the third time, I decided I'd had more than enough. I drew my pistol and blew away one fellow's knee. The other made a move to draw, and I shot him in the chest. The pair of gunshots stopped all movement and all sound in the saloon. The silence was a heavy, ponderous one, like the sensation a person feels when standing in a parlor gawking at a laid-out corpse.

"Don, Lucas," I said. "I guess we're pretty much finished here. Ready to go back to the office and resume our crime-fighting efforts from there?"

The area in front of the bar was littered with bleeding and moaning outlaws. The one I shot in the chest was dead, or at least was showing no signs of life.

Lucas took a bottle from the back of the bar, pulled the cork, sniffed the whiskey, grimaced, and flung the bottle at the back wall, where it shattered. "Hog piss," he commented.

"The good whiskey is somewhere under the bar," I said. Lucas checked for a moment and then exclaimed, "Woooo-weee! Lookit this sumbitch!" He put a Remington double-barreled shotgun on the bar. It'd been cut down so that the barrel wasn't much longer than that of an army Colt. He picked it back up and broke the action, removed the two cartridges, and snapped the weapon shut. "Whoever done this knowed what he was doin'," he said. "He ground down the safety cog so's there ain't no safety at all." He grinned proudly. "This here baby is goin' home with me." Almost as an afterthought, he snagged a bottle of Kentucky bourbon from under the bar.

Don stood in front of me inspecting my face. He winced a bit as he did so. "I'll fetch a bucket of ice," he said. "Your teeth OK?"

"Seems like a couple of the front ones are loose, is all."

"Good. Let's go."

We made our way back to our office, not quite as vigorously as when we were heading to the saloon. Lucas showed little or no damage, but he was limping slightly. Don hadn't been really hurt either; a cut above his right eyebrow that had already stopped bleeding and was crusting over, and a bruise on his jaw. I was the one who took a beating, and I felt somewhat foolish about that.

It seemed like Don read my thoughts.

"Here's the thing, Pound," he said. "You ain't a fistfighter an' never will be. Now, you take a man like Lucas: he's built like a bull, he's dumber than a cow-flop, and he doesn't care a lick if he gets hurt or killed. Same thing kinda applies to me. I ain't as dumb as Lucas, but I'll keep on gettin' up an' fightin' 'til I'm dead."

"Damn right," said Lucas, who apparently wasn't bothered by Don referring to him as dumb.

"You," Don went on, "are a thinker type, an' thinkin' doesn't do any good in a kick-ass fray like today. Plus, you're a gunman."

"I'm not a . . ."

"Bullshit," Don cut me off. "You're real fast an' real good at placin' a slug where you want it to go. That's what I call a gunman."

"But . . ."

"I seen a few gunfights in my day," Don continued. "You ever heard of Frank Leslie—they called him Buckskin Frank?"

"From up around Tombstone, right?"

"Yeah. I seen Frank take down a man who wasn't half bad, but wasn't a gunman. Frank put a round in his left eye an' then two in his chest as he fell. That's a gunman."

I didn't reply.

We sat in the office, me aching a bit, holding a bandana containing some chipped-up ice over my eye. It helped some, but not a lot. Lucas tugged the cork out of the bourbon he'd taken, took a good hit, and handed it to Don. Don sucked much harder than he usually did, and passed the bottle to me. I did that good bourbon justice and gave the bottle to Lucas, continuing the three man circle.

Even though we'd given a good, strong showing of ourselves, we were morose, quiet, vaguely dissatisfied.

Some whooping silver mine workers galloped down the street, probably with pay in their pockets, more than ready to gamble, get drunk, and if enough money happened to be left, purchase the company of a soiled dove.

After the workers went by, the usual over-heated, gritty silence moved in again.

I was damned near asleep when Lucas broke that silence.

"Shit," he said. Strangely, there was dejection in his voice and sadness, too.

"What's the problem?" I asked.

"Well, I know what Don said outside about me not being too bright is true, an' I ain't no school-teacher. But I know men pretty good."

He took a glug from the bottle and then scrambled for words. "Well . . . well . . . dammit, Pound, all we do is every so often whack hell outta some of Powers's men. We cause a little trouble, but not much. It gets old, ya know? Hell, I'd rather be an eagle than a goddamn mosquito."

I was astounded at the metaphor Lucas had just employed. It was stronger than anything I'd read in recent literature. He cleared my confusion: "Sitting Bull said that once."

"Lucas is right," Don said. "We're jus' screwing around and skirmishing. That ain't no way to win a war. An' I got a couple of stills to run, too."

"No, it isn't gonna win a war," I said. "But there's three of us and maybe forty or so of them. Those aren't real good odds."

"Dammit, Pound," Don said vehemently, "we gotta quit slapping wrists and do somethin' that counts." There was a hardness in Don's voice I hadn't heard before. "Powers ain't gonna run 'cause we beat up an' kill a few of his men. He don't give a good goddamn about them—they're easy enough to replace with any saddle bum or outlaw that comes along."

The bottle came to me, and I was about to pass it on when I reconsidered and took three good glugs and let them settle in my gut for a few moments.

"One thing that's to our advantage," I said, "is that there's no more loyalty to that band of cutthroats than there is in a nest of water moccasins." I passed the bourbon to Lucas.

"I can move decently," I said. "Even though I got a solid ass kicking. I'll do some thinking, and then we'll do something that counts—something that makes a difference."

Both my deputies brightened at that. " 'Bout time," Lucas said. "Whatta ya got in mind?"

"I need to think it through a little more. Just keep your drawers up and we'll get something done in Gila Bend," I said.

The fact was I had exactly nothing in mind to accomplish what I'd just told Don and Lucas we would. Every little thought or idea I had came down to one hard fact: the goddamn odds.

"We'll hit 'em hard?" Lucas asked.

"Oh, yeah," I said. "We'll hit 'em hard."

My men were satisfied—at least for now.

Don went to the mercantile to buy some cigarette makings, and Lucas wandered off to wherever it was he decided to go. I suspect he meandered over to visit Miss Tillie Broadman's Gentlemen's Club and Lounge, which was a whorehouse.

I attempted to doze, but my mind was going far too fast for me to nap. I went out back, brushed down my horse, and cleaned out each of his hooves. He poked me with his snout, obviously looking for a treat. I had nothing to give him, but it made me feel good that whoever had owned the buckskin before me cared enough to give him an apple or some such every so often.

I saddled him up and rode out of the end of Main Street—if that's what they called it—and got a couple of miles between me and the town. I checked behind me frequently; no one was following. I cut sharply to the northeast and easily enough found my stash. I took a thousand or so—I didn't bother counting it—and went on with my ride.

Those two good men are going to leave me if we don't do more than punch a few thugs around and shoot one every so often. Don and Lucas needed more, and so did I. I hadn't done a damned thing beyond spend government money, rebuild the office, and sit around sucking beer.

I was thinking as I rode—not that I really cared to, but it was the sort of thing I couldn't control. I was turning everything over in my mind, attempting to find an angle I'd missed or some way to fix things in Gila Bend. I didn't know what the hell to do.

I approached a scattering of fairly large boulders, most higher than the top on my hat as I rode, and many smaller rocks. I would have turned away from it, given it some room, as I rode by. But

I was too far into myself and my problem to pay much attention to the terrain.

My horse picked up his pace without me asking to, and I could feel him tighten, harden, under me. He snorted and shook his head and I took a tighter rein on him. When his head was in a position I could see his face, I saw that his eyes were damned near as big as dinner plates. I gathered yet more rein.

Then I heard what was bothering the horse, and the realization jerked me out of my daze. Rattlesnakes hereabouts grow large, and this boy was large. He was a fat six-footer pulling himself into an attack coil, and his buttons, rattling frenetically, sounded much like a shaken tin can with a handful of pebbles in it.

For a moment, that was the only sound. Then all through the rocks and boulders the same frightening sounds emanated. My horse reared, and I didn't blame him. I gave him the rein he wanted and we hauled ass, putting maybe three-quarters of a mile between us and the rattlers.

It was far too hot to run a horse that hard, but I hadn't asked for the speed; the buckskin had run as he was commanded to by his instinctive fear.

I eased him down to a walk and then stopped. I took a very small sip of water from my full canteen and poured the rest into my hat. The buckskin sucked my Stetson dry in two pulls. I mounted up and continued my aimless ride.

For some reason the relay system of the rattlesnakes stayed in my mind. It was the first time I'd seen or heard such a thing.

I lit a cheroot, but my mouth was too dry to enjoy it. I tossed it aside; sand was all around me, and sand doesn't burn. I decided to go back to Gila Bend. And those damned snakes buzzing to one another stayed on my mind.

I dunno. It seemed one snake told another, and that one told a couple more and pretty soon the whole neighborhood was threatening the intruder, ready to take him on. It seemed like there was something there for me—and there was. It struck me like a kick in the ass, but it brought a big smile to my face.

You see, during and after the war there were a bunch of very hard men in the West. Some ganged up, but the most dangerous of them were loners. There were some pretty strong restrictions to being considered a part of the group of wandering gunmen.

Billy Powers, for instance, would never be involved with these hardcases. He was a coward, a man who had a following of similar cowards riding with him for the booze, money, and women. Not one of them had the balls of a boll weevil.

I'd heard about the group several years ago, when I was partnered up with Zeb Stone. There might be fifty or more—or fewer—of the group. All were killers and all had money on their heads. They weren't what you'd call an affable bunch; they were prone to lynching anyone trying to infiltrate the group, or to use the spy for target practice. Human life—including their own—meant little or nothing to these men.

The point of the group was that they'd help one another to bust out of jail or step into a range war. They scalped a few Indians who paired up with white women, but not too many. In fact, a couple renegade Indians were members.

The way one reached these boys was a wire to St. Bartholomew's Seminary, care of Father Smith, Lubbock, Texas. How this fellow got the message out and disseminated is beyond me, but he did.

I rode the rest of the way into Gila Bend composing my message to the good Father in my mind. I'm not much of a writer, but I think my message was abundantly clear:

> *Pound Taylor needs help retaking the town of Gila Bend. Will pay. Come now. Need is desperate. Outgunned and outmanned.*

It wasn't much on aesthetics, but it said what needed to be said. Payment, by the way, was optional. It wasn't necessarily expected, but it didn't hurt anyone's feelings.

I put my horse in the enclosure behind the jail, rubbed him down good with an empty grain sack, and gave him a flake of hay. Then I went to the tiny telegraph office and sent my wire. The clerk looked at me as if I were a little strange, but said nothing.

I'd been thinking of a cold beer since I sent the wire, which was only a few minutes ago, but still, I wanted that beer. I went into a saloon, bellied up to the bar, and watched the bartender draw a couple of brews. He did a fine job of it, handling his foam-dashing stick with the skill and dexterity of a surgeon. I motioned him over to me. "A cold one," I said, "and let's keep them coming."

He avoided my eyes as he spoke. "I got no cold beer."

"Sure you have," I said. "Those two barrels are packed in ice."

"Don't matter. I still ain't got no cold beer."

A hand fell on my shoulder. "Maybe you don't hear good, but the 'tender says he don't have no cold beer."

I turned to face the speaker. He was a kid, for crissake—maybe twenty-five at the outside. He wore a pair of .45s butt out, in a fancy, nicely tooled gunbelt. His boots looked new—as did his shirt and his denim pants. He wore one of those ridiculous string ties. His face was large and round and looked like it'd be better at laughing than it would be at threatening.

I chose my words carefully. "This isn't going to end up well at all for you, boy. I'll most likely kill you, and I don't want to do that."

"My name's the Yuma Kid," he said, as if that explained something.

"And mine's the Persimmon Porkchop," I said. "And you're pissing me off."

The kid picked up a full shot of whiskey the

bartender had set in front of him and dashed the contents in my face.

"OK," I said. "Out in the street and we'll have at it."

"You betcha," the Yuma Kid said.

There's a feeling that comes to a man when he knows he's in a situation where he can't possibly lose, and this was just such a time. For one thing, this boy would no doubt cross-draw, and by the time he had a good grip on his pistols, he'd be dead. It was possible that he could shoot well, but he wouldn't get an opportunity to do that.

I knew I'd kill this silly pretender, and that made me sad.

I followed him through the batwings. "Lookit, boy," I said quietly, "I'll go my way and you go yours, and no one has to die here, OK?"

"Chickenshit," he snarled.

I took some steps back but let the boy choose his distance.

I don't want to do this.

He walked out about thirty or so paces; the damned sun was directly behind me. The population poured out of the saloon to watch the action.

The boy set himself up. He was crouched slightly—making a cross-draw yet slower and more difficult—with his left boot a foot behind his right.

"I don't want this to happen," I said, "and just look at that, will you?" I'd darted my eyes back to the saloon and the boy's followed mine.

"Ahhh, Jesus," I said.

He brought his eyes back to me, now angrier than before, his face flushing red. "Your goddamn tricks ain't gonna save you," he said.

I sighed audibly.

The flinch of his shoulders told me he was about to draw.

I wanted to give the boy an out, a way to end this thing without me killing him.

In the dime novels, the heroes frequently shoot the weapons out of the bad guys' hands. That, of course, is impossible. I'd learned early on to shoot at the biggest target—that broad rectangle that made up a man's chest and abdomen. There are more than a few fellows in the ground who'd testify I'd done the right thing.

I beat the boy in the draw, just as I knew that I would. The barrel of my Colt automatically flicked up to his chest. I brought it down and fired a round that spurted dirt into the air a foot in front of the boy. My second shot was to take him in the leg. It didn't, and I no longer had a choice.

The boy had finally made his draw and both his pistols were swinging toward me. I put a pair of bullets in his chest. His pistols spun out of his hands and he was thrown backward by the double impact. I holstered my pistol and ran to the Yuma Kid. "I did all I could, but you wouldn't let up. I told you this would . . ."

A gush of frothy blood erupted from his mouth. He spit it away as well as he could. "Next time . . ." he managed to get out.

Paul Bagdon

There won't be a next time, son.

I watched the life seep out of his eyes to leave behind the cold flatness of death. I stood up. The boozers were already going back to the bar. I saw a couple of them eye the boy's .45s and his boots. The mortician and a couple of his flunkies hustled out, carrying a stained stretcher.

I felt as if I was going to vomit. I walked back to my office with bile burning in my throat and mouth—but I wasn't going to give those vultures the opportunity to see me puke. I made it inside to a slop bucket.

Don had brought back several bottles of the whiskey he and his family made, and there was one of them in the big drawer of my rolltop. I pulled the cork with my teeth and hit the bottle hard.

Winter in West Texas is about as subtle as finding a scorpion in your bed.

It generally happens in one of two ways: a late August or early September day is pleasant enough, but there's a sort of a tang to the air—not cold, exactly, but it somehow *smells* different. Then, that night, it snows and winter has arrived and isn't going to go away for a long time.

Usually, horses and dogs get fidgety for no reason, horses pacing in their pastures or nervous in their stalls, and dogs slinking about as if they'd just snatched a roast of beef off a family table and their crime hadn't been discovered yet. Some folks say the birds fly lower, too. That didn't happen this time 'round.

Then, late afternoon, maybe, or into the evening, the wind begins to howl like a wolf bitch in heat and snow seems to come from all directions. Men who've seen this sort of thing before lash a stout rope between their barn and their house, knowing full well if the rope breaks or somehow becomes loose, he's liable to die as he goes to his barn to tend the stock. Lots of farm families keep a special rope that's used for nothing else neatly coiled on a shelf in the barn. That first storm is generally a real pisser; cattle have been known to freeze to death where they stood—and horses, too, for that matter.

The strange thing about a northwester is that the wind comes from all directions at once. That doesn't seem possible, but it is. If the snow breaks long enough to see out a window, a tumbleweed will appear to be zipping back and forth like a ball kicked in a kid's recess game as it's buffeted by the wind.

Quite fortunately, the stove we'd ordered for the office arrived a couple of days before our first winter storm in Gila Bend. "Drop ship" meant precisely that: a couple of railroad employees shoved the stove and its components out a boxcar onto the loading dock in town. We rented a wagon and draft horse from the livery and loaded the stove onto the wagon. The leather springs protested with a shriek and one snapped, listing the wagon slightly to the left. We didn't pay much attention to that. After all, as Lucas said, "Ain't our wagon."

The stove didn't weigh much more than a couple of mountains lashed together. We muscled it inside, grunting and cursing, placing it in the largest open space in the front of the office, which was a few feet from the desk, fairly close to the wall. We faced the loading door toward the office door, figuring it'd make access with armloads of wood easier.

Don took careful measurements of the placement of the stove, using as reference points the walls, door, and so forth. He climbed up onto the roof with his measuring stick and followed the calculations he'd made inside to the smallest part of the roof. Then he whacked a hole in the roof and used a hacksaw to create the opening we needed to run the stovepipe outside. The company had included a nice cap affair for the top of the top of the pipe to keep rain and snow out of fire below in the stove.

Don's measurements were about four inches off, and the pipe wasn't bendable. After damned near busting a gut getting the stove into the office, we needed to move it again.

I should point out here that our temperaments weren't what one would refer to as sweet.

"Ya dumb sonofabitch," Lucas bellowed at Don. "You screwed the pooch on all your fancy-assed measurements an' now we gotta move this goddamn thing again."

Lucas, quite possibly the strongest men I'd ever met, wrapped his arms around the stove. His face became progressively more scarlet as he lifted and shoved, but nothing much was happening. Finally, with his last burst of energy, he skidded the stove a few inches—away from where it needed to be.

"Well," he gasped, "how the hell do you like that?" Then, for his own sanity or revenge or whatever you care to call it, he drew his .45 and shot the stove. The slug didn't even leave a mark on the behemoth, but it did ricochet and punch into our rifle cabinet.

Wordlessly, he holstered his pistol and banged out the door, moving right along to the nearest saloon.

"Anyone in the gin mill who gives him grief is gonna die," Don said.

"I suppose," I said. "Now come on, let's line this thing up before Lucas comes back and breaks a hand punching it."

It took some doing and a whole lot of sweat, but we finally got the stove aligned with the hole in the roof. Don climbed back up and pushed the pipe through the hole and the stove and the pipe mated like a bull and a heifer.

We'd made a deal with a local to supply us with firewood, and there was already a couple cords stacked outside, just beyond the front door.

'Course, we had to try the stove. We loaded her up and used kindling to get the fire going. It started nicely, without an argument. There was some smoke leaking from the seams in the pipe and at the hole in the ceiling, but we glopped those up in good order.

"Darn fine stove," I said.

"She's a real beauty," Don added. After a few minutes, he said, "Gettin' a bit warm in here."

I had to agree. "How do we put it out?" I asked.

Don pondered my question. "Beats hell outta me," he said. "Only experience I've had with stoves is keepin' 'em stoked an' goin', not puttin' 'em out."

"We probably shouldn't have put so much wood in," I said.

"Yeah. Look, she's turnin' red on the sides. That's a hell of a fire."

We looked at one another for a long moment, said "Cold beer" in unison, and then began to move to the door together.

We joined up with Lucas, one of us on each side of him.

"All set?" he asked.

We nodded proudly. "Thing is," I said, "we gave it a try. It works real good, but it's warm in the office just now."

"That means we have to stay here for some time until she burns down that load of wood we stuck in," Don added.

"Well," Lucas said, grinning, "that ain't all bad now, is it?"

A fellow at the bar with a grizzled gray beard that reached his belt buckle remarked to the man next to him, "It's comin', I tell ya. Two days, maybe three, an' you're gonna wish you'd gathered up your beef near the barn. Hell, I already got my rope strung—you should, too."

The other man laughed. "It's too early. Ain't nothin' gonna happen for a couple weeks."

"Bullshit," the ol' boy said, "I recall in oh-one, that . . ."

The younger guy laughed again. *"Fourteen* oh-one?"

"We're ready no matter when the weather comes," Lucas said.

"We'd best be careful with that stove," I said. "Should the office catch on fire, nobody in Gila Bend would do anything but piss on it to put it out."

We continued drinking beer and talking for maybe a bit longer than we should have. As we left, I put a ten-dollar bill on the bar. I'd made it a habit to pay for all my drinks and to tip, as well. Don had, too. Lucas thought we were crazy.

The office was barely habitable, but at least the smeltering-oven effect of the original fire had greatly lessened. Don and I slept in our cells. The office was too hot for Lucas; he slept out in the shelter with our horses.

The next morning was a strange one. The sky to the west was roiling, churning with dark clouds that seemed to collide with one another, separate, and then collide again. There was no lightning and no actual wind in Gila Bend—nothing but a mild breeze.

We stood in front of the office gawking at the sky.

"Well," Lucas said, "it can't be a blizzard—it ain't movin' at all. There's never been no blizzard that didn't move about some."

"It ain't a twister, at least," Don said.

"I don't know what it is. And as long as it stays right out there, I don't much care," I said.

All through the day the mass of dark clouds continued their battle with one another, not moving closer to us or farther away. The breeze hadn't freshened in the least, the temperature remained too damned hot, and no sounds of distant thunder reached us.

I couldn't help recalling the old fellow's words: *It's comin', I tell ya. I already got my safety rope strung. . . .*

None of the stray dogs in town seemed to be concerned about the sky; they went about their daily business of hanging out behind the butcher shop and the restaurant, waiting for scraps.

Our horses were no more or no less content than they ever were, and the business in Gila Bend continued as normal, although those on horseback and pedestrians alike constantly found their eyes scanning the sky.

The next day was a copy of the one before. But those clouds weren't something one could get acclimated to—they kinda lurked in the sky silently, like a cat stalking a mouse.

On the third day, my nerves were raw and my neck a tad sore from constant looking at the sky. "I've had enough of this shit," I told my deputies.

"I'm gonna ride out there a bit closer and see what's going on."

"Might better wait it out," Don said.

"I've been waiting it out for two full days, and not a damned thing has happened. I'm purely sick of waiting it out."

I fetched my horse out of the shelter, saddled him up, and rode out of Gila Bend.

It's difficult to gauge distances in miles when the terrain is so vast and unchanging, but I figured I'd ridden eight, maybe ten miles. We cut a little stream and we both drank and I lit a cheroot.

The strange thing was that I didn't appear to be getting any closer to those damned clouds. The temperature may have dropped very slightly, but then again, maybe it hadn't. The whispering little breeze in town seemed to have followed me.

I have to say that nothing like this had ever happened to me before or since. I was riding along, relaxed in the saddle, giving some thought to lighting a cheroot, when I heard a train coming—a train that was very close to me. But there were no railroad tracks around. Before I could find the logic in that, the storm descended on me in all its howling, wretched, screaming power.

It was like a theater curtain of pure white suddenly dropped down on all sides of me and my horse—but these curtains allowed the wind and snow to lash at us, scaring hell out of my horse—and me, too, I guess. My horse spun and reared a couple of times, but I kept him under control. The thing is, his spin disoriented me; I couldn't tell up from down, much less the four directions. Absolutely nothing was visible except a blinding barrage of white. My Stetson was snapped off my head and then gone.

I didn't really notice the cold at first, probably because I was too confused and frightened by this monster that'd attacked me. I'd been riding in denim pants, a work shirt, a leather vest, and boots—hardly winter wear.

My horse danced under me wanting a command, a direction from me, but I had none to give.

The snow wasn't in flake form—it was more like tiny ice pellets that stung bare flesh and through my shirt. I think I mentioned quite a bit earlier that I had absolutely no skill or feel for directions. That's much of the reason I ended up in Gila Bend. Then, my lack was an inconvenience; now it was a matter of life and death.

I couldn't see the sun. I had no way to choose the direction to Gila Bend. I knew there were stone outcroppings somewhere ahead, but I didn't know in which direction.

I'd experienced fear before. Waiting to be hanged is a constant fear that permeates every thought, every move, every breath. I'd been trapped in a bank once, surrounded by half a town of men with rifles, pistols, and shotguns. I fell into an empty well as a kid. I've faced gunmen who just might be a tiny bit better than me.

But nothing was ever like this.

My horse was becoming more and more fractious, ready to start bucking for real, or rolling over on me, to get rid of me so that he could run. I gave him some rein and he charged ahead, stopped suddenly, set out in another direction, and then stopped, his body trembling. He didn't know where the hell we were either, and he hadn't been in Gila Bend long enough for the shelter to establish itself as a safe place.

I kept him moving to keep the pair of us from freezing to death right where we stood. *Why the hell didn't I listen to that ol' coot? He knew what he was talking about. If I'd paid more attention to his warning, I wouldn't be out here killing myself and a damn fine horse.*

The train sound was constant, although for a few moments at a time, it'd sound like a large stream carrying winter runoff—a whooshing, hissing sort of racket.

I calculated it this way: I had a choice of four main directions. I didn't know which one would bring us anywhere near Gila Bend. And 'somewhere near' was no good—I might as well be standing right where I was as I'd be a mile from town, if this storm was moving that way, and I'm pretty sure that it was.

My face was numb and so were my hands. I managed to tie my reins together so I could rein with one hand and stick the other one under my arm to maybe loosen it up a little. Then I veered off to my left and booted my horse into a clumsy jog.

Actually, this isn't all that bad. It must be warming

up some, because I don't feel nearly as cold as I had . . . when . . . a day ago? An hour ago?

It didn't make any difference because it was definitely warming nicely. I looked down at my hands to see if I was reining, but I couldn't see them. I knew I was still mounted because I was moving without walking. That made laugh, but the laughing hurt my mouth.

What I needed and what my buckskin needed was a rest—a place where we could hunker down and get some sleep and by the time we awakened, all this train noise and snow would be melted away. If we curled up together, we'd keep each other warm as long as we needed to until it was summer-warm outside. I laughed again and didn't mind the hurt. Why the hell didn't I think of that yester—

Two sounds jerked me back from my dream. I didn't know what they were—my head wasn't working real well—but in maybe a couple of minutes later I heard the two sounds again, and they registered. Someone was firing a rifle.

I had a rifle in my saddle scabbard and reached for it. I couldn't tell if it was there or not. It seemed like there was something, but my hands refused to grasp whatever it was. I gave up on the reins and jammed both hands under the opposite armpit. If I could get even a small semblance of sensation back, I was pretty sure I could haul out the rifle, work the lever, and fire it.

I started to drift again and caught myself. I yelled as loud as I possibly could. I couldn't hear anything over the train, but I knew sound was coming out of me, or was pretty sure it was.

I began to feel a very remote tingle in my hands. It wasn't strong enough to be called a sensation, but it was something. I pulled my hands out of my shirt and banged them together, rubbing them hard, as if washing them. The tingling became very slightly more pronounced. I kept on washing, kept on shouting.

Then I tried it—I tried to clutch the .30-30, cock it, and fire.

I got my left hand on what I was pretty certain was the stock and tugged it out and toward me. I reached for the lever with my right hand, which hit my left hand and the rifle tumbled away into the impenetrable whiteness.

The only option I had left was my pistol. My right hand was so used to the exact position of that .45 that even frozen solid, my palm would go to it. I needed to do something fast, because I didn't think we were moving any longer, and I kept flashing in my mind on the bed I'd slept in as a kid. It was like my bed was right in front of me and all I needed to do was to . . .

My palm found the grips and my right finger slid into the trigger housing. I struggled the Colt out of my holster and attempted to fire it off to the side. My goddamn finger refused that one silly, half-assed move. I think I screamed again and at that time I must have exerted enough pressure with my trigger finger. The Colt fired. I did it again—fired—and then waited. I fired twice, quickly. That left me with two live rounds. There was no way in the world I'd be able to remove a cartridge from my gunbelt and get it into the .45's cylinder.

I pointed the barrel upward and jerked the trigger twice.

This is it. I can go to my bed now.

Something large bumped in to my horse. Then there was a voice: "You stupid bastid! What the hell are you doing out here? Jesus, waddan idjit."

Chapter Six

I could feel someone doing something to the front of my saddle, but I couldn't see the person or what he was doing. I wasn't at all sure whether my eyes were open or shut and frosted closed, but I suspected the latter.

A cup of booze magically began prodding at my mouth, pushing through the accumulated ice and frozen nose-drippings. I drank it down, whoever it was slowly lifting the cup so that I didn't lose a drop, and so that I wouldn't have to tilt my head back.

After that, it seemed like a long time passed with nothing happening except the train going by, the cold, and the total whiteness of everything.

My horse began to move. I reached for the reins but couldn't find them with my numbed hands.

Had the voice shouting in my ear been a dream? Had the whiskey been a dream? I didn't think so; I could still taste the liquor. But was that sensation of taste a dream, as well? I felt like my horse was walking, but I couldn't be real sure. Riding is done with the butt and the legs, and mine were numb—as if they were frozen solid.

Whatever was happening went on forever. Something was wrapped around me, but it accomplished nothing. The miniscule glow from the alcohol was long gone—if it'd existed at all.

I fought my way to consciousness and found nothing but pain. A million tiny fire arrows had been shot into my body, each inflicting its own private pain. I thought that I may be on fire, but opened my eyes and saw that I wasn't.

I took me several moments to figure out where I was. Everything shimmered in my vision—nothing was clear. There were two faces looking down at me. One, I think, was Don. The other I didn't recognize. A hand lifted my head and a cup of broth that was maybe half bourbon was held to my lips. I drank it all, and within moments, I was again asleep.

When I woke up the next time, the faces were gone and so was most of the shimmering in my vision. The fire arrows had turned to blunt pins, but they were bearable. I looked around. I was on the floor of the office very close to the stove, covered with a robe or blanket of some sort. I think I was nude. Heat poured from the stove like water through a breached dam, and I reveled in it, my body sucked it up like desert sand sucks rain.

A face peered down at me. "He's awake again," Don's voice said.

"My horse . . ." I managed to croak out.

"Lucas has been rubbing the hell out of him for

the past few hours, Pound, and giving him only warm water to drink. His lower lip is frostbit some, but not too bad. He's gonna be fine."

"How'd I . . . get . . . here?"

"A fella brought you in. Says he put a loop around your saddle horn and kinda dragged you and your horse in to Gila Bend. I'll tell you this: he's one tough sumbitch."

"Who . . . ?"

"Wouldn't say," Don said. "He said he seen your badge, otherwise he woulda left you 'til spring meltdown. Says you were lookin' for him."

Don held another mug of that bourbon broth to my mouth and I sucked it down. It eased my voice considerable. I noticed that the train sound was still roaring outside but it was muffled.

"Storm bad?" I asked.

"Oh, yeah the storm is bad. Nobody seen the damned thing coming after that first day when the sky was dark. Caught lots of folks with stock out in pastures. A couple wagonloads of mine workers aren't accounted for yet. Couple kids out playing ain't been home yet—and probably never will be. Hell, there's better'n three feet of snow out there, Pound." His voice changed, became bitter. "Only ones who did OK are Billy Powers and his crew. They stayed in their saloons drinkin', whorin', an' playin cards. There's a few horses standin' out at the hitchin rails froze solid."

I waited a few moments before speaking. "The man who brought me in—where'd he go? Is he coming back here to the office?"

"I sent him over to the hotel. He wouldn't go there until he got his horse down to the livery an' in a stall and rubbed good. Then I guess he went to the hotel."

"He saw my star, is what he said?"

"Yeah. He said somethin' about a deal an' needin' some cash money, too."

"Oh." *So the word has gotten out to some of the right people.*

"Don, you have any long johns I could borrow? Are my clothes dry yet?"

"Yes to both questions. We ran a rope over the top of the stove to dry your stuff, and I'll fetch some long johns outta my cell."

It was while I was dressing that the infernal itching started. It was that of a mosquito bite times a million. Jesus, how I itched! I suppose it was merely skin coming back to life after it'd damned near frozen. I tried not to attack the itches, but had little luck. Those things demanded to be scratched.

Don came back with the long johns and the tin of hoof dressing from our shelter. "Look," he said, "I figured this itch would slide in on you. Just put a little bit of this stuff on your fingers and rub it into your skin."

"Damn, Don, I'm gonna smell like a used-up horse."

Don grinned. "Up to you. I know this works. I didn't realize you were going to a damned cotillion tonight to dance with those purdy Southern ladies and then escort one out on the porch or maybe to behind the stables . . . but you're right, Pound. No lady in her right mind would care to spread her legs for a fellow who smells like a hoof."

I didn't have much to say about that.

"I'm gonna walk out a bit while you do what you need to do. I wanna check how much damage the town has taken on."

I did as Don instructed and found that the hoof dressing worked as he said it would. I stood there nude and stupid, globs of hoof dressing on each hand, rubbing it on.

It worked—and it worked fast and well.

I was tugging on my boots and reveling in the non-itch of my skin when the office door swung open, bringing in a frantic burst of snow, wind, temperature low enough to freeze a brass monkey's eggs clean off—and what looked like a giant, long-coated prairie dog.

He stood in the open doorway looking at me, his eyes the only part of his face visible under the pelt of whatever animal he was under. A pair of bandoleers of ammunition crossed his chest, and he held a .30-30 loosely in his right hand, the rifle's action covered by the fur mitten he wore. The inch-long talons of the mittens made it pretty clear that he didn't purchase the mittens at a mercantile.

"You Pound?" he asked in a voice that wasn't low and threatening as I'd expected, but that of a normal rancher.

"You wanna close that door?" I said.

"You wanna answer my question, ya little pis-sant?"

"I'm Pound," I said.

He shut the door. He took a step closer to the stove and pushed his hood back, showing a narrow face with eyes set too closely together. His long mustache continued past both sides of his mouth and hung down an inch or better on either side of his chin.

"It's a good thing you *are* Pound," he said. "Otherwise I'd have wasted a whole lot of time draggin' some goddamn ribbon clerk back to his town. It's nippy out there," he added, "and some breezy, too."

"Who are you?" I asked. "What's your name?"

"Don't make no difference."

"The thing is, I need . . ."

"You sent a wire," he said. "You must be worth-while—if you ain't, you wouldn't have knowed where to send it."

"I sure need some help . . ."

"You got a single dollar you can spare?" he said, cutting me off.

That confused me. "Sure. But what's a dollar going to . . ."

He pulled off his left mitten with his teeth. One of the talons left a scratch next to his nose. In his bare palm rested a compass—more like a kid's toy than a navigation instrument.

"This little fella saved your bacon," he said.

"Yours, too," I said.

"Maybe—and maybe not."

"I'll get me one of those compasses and keep it with me," I said.

"That'd make some good sense."

Lucas came in from the back, stomping his boots and slapping his hands together.

"The horses are good," he said. "We got nuff hay for a couple-three days." He stomped his boots a few more times to get some sensation in his feet. "I tell you, Pound, this storm for sure calls for . . ."

He stopped speaking when he saw we had a guest.

". . . calls for a friendly beverage—maybe two— no?" The man with no name finished Lucas's sentence.

"Right." Lucas grinned and held out his hand to the stranger to shake. The other man ignored it.

"Ain't what you'd call real social-like, are you?"

"No."

"You got a name?"

"Jake'll do for now."

"That drink still sound good, Jake?"

Jake nodded as Don came in the front door. "I walked as far as the mercantile. It an' all the other stores are closed up tight. The saloons are up and runnin' an' doin' lots of business—most all of it to Powers's men, 'cause they don't pay for drinks or women."

"This Powers—he's the one we're after?" Jake asked.

"An' his collection of shitheels, too, o'course," Lucas added. To Don, he said, "This fella here is Jake. He's come to give us a hand."

Lucas pulled open the deep drawer of the roll-top and took out a clear, unlabeled bottle.

Jake grimaced. " 'Shine the best you boys can do?" He looked and sounded like he was asking if we always put cowshit in our oatmeal.

"Taste it," I said.

Jake took the bottle, plucked the cork, sniffed the whiskey, then took a drink of it. His face lit up with a large smile. "Jesus," he said. He reached his hand out to shake with Lucas. He also shook with me and with Don.

"You boys is OK," he said. "I know this didn't come from no general store or gin mill. It's as sweet as a virgin's teat."

Lucas took a step closer to Jake. "I been purely admirin' your coat," he said. "What critter'd you skin her off of? Looks like a bear, but that color . . ."

"He was a grizzly, OK," Jake said. "But you boys know what an albino is?

"Sure," I said.

"Yeah," Don said, "of course."

"It's a town somewheres in New Mexico, ain't it? I can't say I been there, but I know what it is," Lucas said.

To his credit, Jake didn't laugh. "You're thinkin' of Albuquerque, Lucas. Easy mistake to make. But, see, an albino is an animal that's pure white, an' more likely'n not, has pink eyes. Anyways, this here coat isn't from a full albino—his coloring got a little screwed up when he was still in his mama."

"How'd you take him?" I asked. "He musta been big."

"He stood an honest seven feet, he did, an' he was as ornery as a sack fulla rattlers. I didn't want to shoot him an' put a hole or two in his pelt. So I got up on his back and slashed his throat. You'd be right surprised how much blood there is in a big bear."

"A albriono," Lucas mused. "Was his blood white, too?"

"It's 'albino,' an' no, his blood was as red as your'n an' mine."

For some moments, no one said anything. Jake hadn't yet relinquished the bottle. He took another good hit and passed the booze to Don. "Awful fine whiskey," he said.

Don didn't seem to have much to say. He wore a wrinkled-brow, worriedlike face damned near every time I saw him. I couldn't figure him out.

Jake turned to me. "Look," he said, "these two gents are right in the middle of this shit with Powers an' gettin' you a pardon, right?"

"Yeah," I said. "They are. I've told them—and I didn't make any promises or twist any arms.

"Well, then," Jake said, "you boys are pards, right?"

"Yeah," Lucas answered.

"Kinda," Don said.

"No," I said. "We work together an' we cover each other's backs, but we're not pards. Zeb Stone was the last partner I ever care to have."

"Why?" Jake asked. "Robbin' banks is risky. I

Paul Bagdon

knew ol' Zeb an' that crazy family of his, an' I know Zeb Stone feared nothin' an' no one. You think Zeb was surprised when he got shot up at that bank? Hell no! It's the business he was in. He's the one who chose it. He'd want you to have a partner."

Jake was rattling me a bit. "Let's let it go for now," I said.

"Fair nuff," he said. "Just now I'm wonderin' if you boys could spare me another little taste of that fine, fine whiskey?"

Late that night I overheard a brief conversation between Don and Lucas.

"Pa can handle it for crissake," Lucas said. "It ain't like the bottoms are gonna burn through. Damn, you worry like a woman, Don—but I reckon it's up to you to decide where you need to be. Don't make us no never mind. A man, he does what he's gotta do."

I knew that something was coming up between Don and me, and I had a real strong suspicion what it was.

The storm continued past the point where it became tedious and monotonous—then it kept on going. Any storm I ever lived through had one constant, one thing that always happened: the wind that was driving it abated. This sonofabitch wind, however, screamed the second and third day like a scalded cat, and the snow continued to come in horizontally.

Lucas, Don, and I saw to our horses—smashing

the ice in their troth so they could drink, making certain their standing area was mucked out, and checking them to make sure they weren't chewing on each other. Horses get bored just as men do, and a relief to boredom in both men and horses was fighting. There were no problems in the shelter thus far, however.

Jake made it down to the livery every ten or twelve hours to check on his horse. He did it by moving along the street, tight to the buildings, feeling doors and windows to orient himself. The livery was way the hell out at the end of the street, but he made it out and back every time. On one of his trips he brought back a deck of playing cards from his saddlebag.

I'd rather have a tooth pulled than play poker— or any card game—but I enjoyed watching.

Don, Lucas, and Jake played. Lucas was the aggressive one—he'd heavy-bet a hand that a three-year-old would have folded. Don was conservative in his playing—he'd ditch a hand unless he was fairly certain he could win with it. Jake was yet more reckless than Lucas, but he won more hands than his opponents did.

We were drinking bar whiskey—the supply Lucas had brought back from his home was long gone. It was crypt-quiet in the office, except for the slap of cards. Outside the storm continued, but we didn't really hear it, any more than a man who lives on a lake hears the constant waves.

I was just about dozing off on the floor not far from the stove when Lucas stood and swept the cards and cash from the desktop and bellowed, "I seen what you just done, you sonofabitch! You're cheatin'!"

Jake was incredulous. "Why, sure I am. Ain't you boys?"

I got to my feet in a hurry. I didn't need two of my men pounding the piss outta each other.

"You don't cheat against friends," Lucas said.

Jake smiled. "I cheat against everybody—every goddamn body—'cause if I didn't, I might lose."

I moved closer to stand in front of Lucas. His hands weren't clenched into fists and that, I thought, was a good sign.

Jake said, "I don't want none of that money on the floor. You boys split it. I was jus' playin' for fun, is all."

"I might have killed you," Lucas said.

Jake grinned. "Sure," he laughed. "Right when hogs start to nest in trees. Lemme show you boys somethin'," he said, as he shoved his chair back. He took a .45 from a shoulder holster under his bear coat.

"That ain't nothin' . . ." Lucas began.

"Hush now." Jake made a quick, short motion with his right hand—a flick type of thing—and a long, narrow-bladed knife appeared in his hand. He threw it at a Wanted poster on the far wall, pinning the criminal directly between the eyes. Jake moved his left hand and an over-and-under Derringer magically rested comfortably in his palm. "I killed me a deer once with this baby," he said. "The recoil on the sumbitch would knock down a fat bull buffalo, but it sure does the job." He placed the Derringer on the desktop along with the other weapons he'd drawn. He pulled a short, double-edged throwing knife from his right boot and another from his left and put them on the desk.

"Damn," Lucas said. "The man's a walkin' arsenal." To Jake, he said, "Can I have a look-see at that little over-an'-under? I ain't doubtin' your say-so, but I never seen a Derringer that could stop a chipmunk. I'd like to take her outside, squeeze a shot off."

Jake's grin became broader. "I figured the sheriff here"—he nodded at me—"would be the one to see if I was lyin' 'bout that gun."

"Makes no difference to me what that pistol can or can't do," I lied.

In truth I was just about to ask to take it outside when Lucas spoke up.

Jake took the Derringer from the desk and handed it to Lucas.

Lucas hadn't gotten a good look at the piece until it was in his hand. He whistled a long note. "Lookit the bore on this goddamn thing! A fella could damn near fire a twelve-pound cannonball through either barrel."

"Watch yer ass," Jake suggested. "There ain't no safety on it. The pull is heavy, but still . . ."

Lucas nodded. "I'll watch her," he said.

He didn't bother with his heavy coat or mittens

or any other outdoor clothing. He walked out the door and pulled it shut behind him. Nothing happened for maybe two minutes. It seemed like the wind had gotten suddenly stronger and more intense for that bit of time, but that was probably because we were listening so hard.

There were two terribly loud explosions so close together they sounded almost like a single report. In a moment, Lucas shoved the door open and reentered the office. His shirt and pants in front were snowless, but his shoulders, back, and pants in back were encrusted with white. He'd been literally knocked on his ass.

"How much you want for her?" Lucas said.

"Ain't for sale."

"Gimme the name of the gunsmith who made 'er for ya, then."

"He's dead," Jake said, holding his hand out for the Derringer.

Lucas handed the gun over reluctantly.

Jake reloaded the pistol with 44-50 brass-jacketed cartridges, the same round the Sharps buffalo gun fired. "I'll tell you what," Jake said, "should I get killed in what we're doin' here, you can have her. Fair nuff?"

"Hot damn!" Luas exclaimed. "I purely 'preciate that! Hot damn," he repeated.

If Lucas had been a lesser man, I might have suspected him of planting a slug in Jake's head when our battles with Powers got intense, but he wasn't a lesser man. Jake must have known that, or he wouldn't have made the offer he put in front of Lucas.

The storm kind of slunk away like a whipped dog—tail between its legs, all its fight gone—and disappeared, all in the course of a single night. We checked on our horses, which were showing signs of acute boredom.

Don's horse had begun cribbing, a strange habit extremely bored horses invented. A cribbing horse will lock his front teeth into the top plank of a stall and rock slightly, his teeth gripping tight. They'll do this for hours at a time. There's at least a couple of problems cribbing causes. For one thing, they make the stall plank look like hell, with a half-moon shape maybe two or three inches deep every so often along its length. Second, and much more important since planks are cheap, is the fact that the damned fools will swallow the splinters they chew free, and those splinters can pierce the horses' throat or gut, and then the owner is left with a thousand pounds or so of dead horse to haul out of a stall and plant somewhere.

The morning of the night the storm ended Don took his horse down to the livery and turned him out into the five- or six-acre pasture there. Of course it was all covered with better'n a couple of feet of snow, but the horse had some space to flounder around and buck and kick and burn off some energy. Later that day, I took my buckskin down there, too. He was as edgy as a nun in a cathouse, and he charged out into the drifts as soon as I set him free.

The next day was almost fifty degrees, which meant that all that snow began to melt. Main Street in Gila Bend—such as it was—became a sea of mud and clay, almost impassable on horseback and completely impassable to freight wagons hauling to the mercantile essentials, such as barrels of beer, and supplies, such as ammunition, smoking tobacco, whiskey, lamp fuel, and so forth.

We left our horses in the stable pasture—they weren't much good as riding stock, and they enjoyed being out and rolling in the mud, digging their shoulders in, and grunting like sows. The blacksmith at the livery was doing a hell of a business. Mud and clay sucks off shoes just as a leech sucks blood. Anyone stupid enough to attempt to ride any distance deserved the smith's jacked up prices. He tried to charge Jake two dollars to reset a shoe. Jake told the smith he'd bring a shoe to white hot in the forge and then stick it up the blacksmith's ass. The smith did the reset for his usual price of fifty cents.

The third day, while the snow was still melting, a couple of men walked into town. They looked like bad news for no particular reason. They were dressed like saddle tramps, probably smelled like tubs of shit, and simply slogged along down the street. Still, there was a chill around them— an aura of violence.

I'd been standing at the office window, watching the two men. Don was sitting over in the corner. Jake, half drunk and playing his harmonica with all the skill of a goddamn chimpanzee, sat behind my desk. I called him to the window.

"You know them?" I asked.

"Of course I know them," Jake said. "You couldn't find a crazier pair of partners anywhere in the West—they're both loony. Big Nose—the one who's a bit taller—has taken over fifty scalps, mostly from white men, white women, and white babies. Hairy Dog—the other one—is a hell of a shot with either a pistol or rifle. He's some ugly— he has a dog face and more hair to him than a good beaver pelt. Injuns don't usually grow much hair—but ol' Dog, he's like a goddamn bear rug."

"Do they speak English?"

"Why sure, Pound. They talk damned near as good as me. They might slide in a bit of Injun-ish every so often, but that ain't no never mind. It ain't the words as well as the order they put them in. Ya know?"

"What the hell do they want in Gila Bend?"

Jake laughed. "You ain't quite figured this out, Pound. These two loons got the telegram. They're part of us now, like their style or not."

"Ahh, shit," I said. "How am I supposed to control these two screwups?"

"Well, you can't. You try to an' one or the other will kill you." He paused there for a long moment. "Uhh, one other thing, Pound. Sometimes they eat the heart and the liver of their victims, but those are usually warriors beat in a battle. I ain't heard of them doin' it recently, but I thought you'd like to know."

"Sweet Jesus," I said, almost to myself.

I turned from the window, mad. "I didn't sign on for crazies like these two. Hell, I'm inclined to take them down right now with one of our .30-30s and forget 'bout the sonsabitches."

"They're comin' this way," Jake said. "If you're gonna try a play, you'd best do it now. If you ain't, shut the hell up an' 'member what I told you."

I crossed over to the rifle cabinet and pulled out a .30-30. It wasn't loaded, but I filled it and jacked a round into the firing chamber.

The Indians pushed open the door and stepped inside. I noticed that they immediately spread apart, making themselves two targets instead of one. Big Nose said, "You lookin' to die with that toy in your hands?" He let his right hand drop quite casually to his side, then raised a cutoff 12-gauge from beneath his coat. The weapon was on a nicely constructed swivel. "You figure you're goin' to screw with us, pale man?"

"I'll tell you what I figure: There's two men with me here. Maybe I'll get a shot off into one of you and maybe not. But these two boys will kill you right where you stand."

Hairy Dog's solemn face broke into a huge smile, and he moved to embrace Jake. "Why damn me to hell!" he all but shouted. "Jake, it's a gift from the gods to meet up with you again."

Jake and the Indian hugged, slapping each other

on the back. "You 'member," Hairy Dog said, "when you'n me shot our way outta that jail in Durango?"

"Oh, yeah I do," Jake said. "Your crazy sumbitch partner got us a couple of chopped-down 10 gauges. Jesus! That first round I fired damn near busted my wrist."

"That Marshall, he was handy," the Indian said. "You done right in dropping him first. But you white men, you got no strength. You moaned and carried on for a couple of days about your hand. 'Course that was the one you pleasured your own-self with."

"I hear you Injuns screw lots of goats—an' the goats walk away thinkin' they've been bit by a mosquito."

They laughed and embraced again. "Big Nose," Jake said over Hairy Dog's shoulder, "you're lookin' right good for an ol' man."

"Just old enough to kick your scrawny ass, white boy."

Jake stepped away from Hairy Dog. "I got two friends here," he said to the Indians. He pointed at me. "This here's the sheriff. His name is Pound. And this feller's name is Don," he said, nodding at Don. "They're both good men, an' you can trust 'em with your life."

Indians aren't real big on shaking hands, and neither approached Don or me.

"Who is the enemy in this town?" Hairy Dog asked.

"Fellow named Billy Powers," I said. "He's

taken over Gila Bend. I get a full pardon if I take back the city."

Hairy Dog grunted. "What do we get?"

"A thousand each."

"Cash money?"

"Cash money."

"How many men has this Billy Powers? Are they good fighters?"

"About forty, give or take a few. Some are gunmen, but most are screwups from the war—drunks, killers, and so forth."

"I must wire the good Father," Hairy Dog said, "tell him to send no more men. We have enough here. Where is the wire office?"

"I dunno about us having enough men," I said. "The odds are lousy. You and Big Nose even things up a bit, but . . . well . . . forty men is a lot."

"Not so many," Hairy Dog said. "And we have no need to fight them all at once."

"We'll go to the wire office now. Your store, it has tobacco for smoking?"

"Sure," I said.

The Indians left without further speaking. "This ought to be good," Jake said, moving to the window. "I suspect that the ol' goat who owns the mercantile won't do business with Injuns."

Don and I moved in behind and next to Jake and watched Hairy Dog and Big Nose trudge down the street to the mercantile. They went inside and for a long moment, nothing happened. Then the owner of the store sailed through his front show window in a glistening rain of shards and bits of window glass. A minute later the two Indians walked out, each with a fat paper sack of tobacco and each smoking a shiny new pipe.

The three of us laughed. "I guess maybe he'll be more open to Injun trade now," Don said.

Word of what happened at the mercantile must have spread rapidly. When the Indians took a room at the hotel, not a word was said, and the same applied to the restaurant. They got lots of attention as they ate, though. They had no use for forks, and they used their own knives on anything that needed to be cut. When Hairy Dog picked up a handful of mashed potatoes and shoved them into his mouth, there was an audible gasp from the other diners. Both Indians picked up their steaks and gnawed away at them, grunting, grease running down their chins. There was a bottle of whiskey on the table. Neither man bothered using a glass. When Hairy Dog removed a cud-sized, partially chewed piece of steak from his mouth, inspected it carefully, and then tossed it over his shoulder, the few diners who'd remained, left, many with half-consumed meals on their plates.

I guess because they had nowhere else they wanted to go, Hairy Dog and Big Nose returned to the office. The five of us sat around smoking, not saying much, listening to horses slopping by outside.

"This ain't fightin'," Big Nose said. "This is settin' like an ol' granny warmin' her ass by the fire. Me an' Dog, we come to fight, not to set."

Hairy Dog nodded. "Maybe you give us our money now an' we go on our way." He said it as a statement, not as a question.

"You know," Jake said, "what Nose said is right. We ain't treatin' our new guests real well. How's about we take them on a tour of the saloons in town—kinda let them get acquainted with some of Powers's boys." Of course, Jake knew what doing that would precipitate, and I noticed a pleased little glint in his eyes.

"Sounds like a good idea to me," Don said.

"Me too," I agreed. "But first . . ." I walked to the rifle closet and handed .30-30s to Jake and Don and took one for myself. I looked at Nose. "We don't need no rifles," he said. Dog nodded.

"Fine with me," I said. "Come on, boys—let's load 'em up an' keep 'em loaded from now on." The rifle I held was already fully loaded with a round in the chamber—it was the one I thought I might use to pick off the two Indians.

There were five saloons in little Gila Bend. It didn't make much difference which one we visited first. I set out but Jake grabbed my shoulder. "It's a sign of disrespect to make the Injuns follow you. We either walk in a straight line or one of them takes the lead."

"OK," I said. "Big Nose, how about we go over to that saloon, the one with the piano playing?"

Nose took the lead with Dog right behind him, and we squished and slopped over the street behind Dog, following him like baby ducks follow their mothers. The piano stopped and so did all conversation when the two Indians pushed through the batwings. They walked to the bar.

"Whiskey," Dog said.

The bartender shook his head. "We don't serve no redskins in here, chief."

Don, Jake, and I spread out behind the Indians, several feet between us.

Hairy Dog grinned at Big Nose. "He says they don't serve no Indians in here."

"Why's that?" Nose asked.

"Why's that?" Dog asked the bartender.

"'Cause all of ya are stinkin' goddamn savages—animals 'stead of people." He was already reaching behind the bar for the scatter gun that was no doubt there.

Nose pushed his coat aside and swiveled his cut-down 10-gauge and fired at the bottles behind the bar. Booze and glass spewed in all directions, like shrapnel from an exploding canister round. The bartender, shocked, stood halfway up, not yet clutching the scattergun. Hairy Dog reached over the bar and slammed the top of the 'tender's head with the butt of his Colt. The man went down into a puddle of booze and broken glass.

Big Nose put a hand on the bar and vaulted over it. He strode to the end of the bar where his 10-gauge hadn't done much damage, selected a bottle, pulled the cork with his teeth, and took a long drink. He tossed the bottle to Dog, who also did it justice. Jake had a drink. Don and I abstained for the moment. I was more concerned about the men at the card tables than I was in having a drink, and I'd turned toward them, hand on the grips of my Colt.

"You boys be sure to tell Billy what happened here," I said. To my men, I said, "C'mon, let's get outta this dump."

Big Nose led us to the batwings. I noticed that Jake snagged a fresh bottle on the way out.

The next nearest gin mill was three storefronts down, on the same side of the street. We trooped down there, my mind again forming an image of a mother duck being followed by her babies. Outside the second saloon we ran into Lucas and I introduced him to Dog and Nose. One of the thugs must have run out the back of the first place we hit because just as Nose was about to shove a batwing, a slug dug into the wood frame next to his head. Most of the tables were tipped—being used for cover—and a genuine fusillade followed that first shot at Nose. We stood outside, sort of bunched up, wondering what the hell they were shooting at.

Hairy Dog held his hand out to me. "This pisses me off, standing out here like women. Borrow me your rifle." I had no idea what he was going to do, but I wasn't about to question him. "Is it fully loaded?" he asked.

"Plus one in the pipe," I said.

Dog looked up at Big Nose for a moment, their eyes locked, and it was as if a sort of communication the others couldn't hear took place between them. Nose grinned and nodded.

Dog crouched and then launched through the batwings like a swimmer diving into a pond, except that he was getting off shots that made some difference, gauging from the screams and yells from inside. Nose followed his friend, shotgun in one hand, an army Colt in the other. He, too, did some damage.

We followed the Indians. The interior of the saloon was thick with blue-white smoke and the metallic smell of blood. Shouts, curses, and more screams weren't as loud as the barking of our pistols and the hollow, concussive roar of the shotgun—that of Big Nose and that of a man crouched at the end of the bar. He raised up a bit to fire and I gunned him down.

Two outlaws were hunkered down behind a table, firing rapidly. Jake smiled. "Watch this," he shouted to Don. He made the quick motion that placed the Derringer in his hand and fired twice at the table. Almost as if it'd been choreographed, a man fell to each side. Most of one outlaw's head was gone; the other had a hole in his chest large enough to drive a wagon through.

"I'll give you a thousand dollars for that gun," Lucas said.

"Ain't for sale," Jake answered.

The firing from inside the saloon ceased. Dog took a bottle from the bar and poured its contents on the floor, emptying it. Then he did the same with another. He stuck a match and tossed it at the edge of the puddle of whiskey. There was a loud *whooomph* sound, and orange flames leapt from the floor and licked at everything around them.

"Nice touch," I said to Hairy Dog.

"We could stand here and drop them as they run out," Nose said.

"No," I said. "Let's go on down the street and visit another gin mill."

"I could use a drink," Jake said.

"It's a rare damned time when you couldn't use a drink," Lucas said.

Jake thought that over. "Yeah," he finally said. "I guess you could be right on that. Don't make me want a drink no less, though."

Our parade set out again, stopping in front of a smaller saloon than the other two had been. Nose jacked a round into the rifle he carried and began to say something when Hairy Dog tackled him—hard—carrying both men several feet to where they landed in the mud. The shot from the roof stuck where Big Nose had been standing.

"Goddamn, that makes me mad," Nose said. "Tryin' to ambush a man like that. Dog, you see jist where he was?"

"No. I seen the glint on the barrel of his rifle right up there, to the right of the door."

"Well, damn," Nose said. "I tell you what: this one ain't goin' down easy." There were a couple of cow horses at the hitching rail, standing pastern deep in muck and mud. Big Nose unfastened the throwin' rope from one horse, formed a quick loop, and hurled it over the chimney extension that stuck up on the roof. He handed his rifle to

Hairy Dog, slid a twelve-inch bowie knife out of his boot, and climbed that rope as easily as he'd walk up a few stairs. We couldn't see much of anything because there was a wall across the roof, kind of a false front to make the place appear larger—maybe two full stories.

There were a couple of rifle shots in quick succession, and then one more—and then a gurgling scream that sent a chill the length of my spine. A moment later, the rifleman's head arced up and splashed down in the street.

"Didn't take his scalp," Dog commented. "I kinda figured he would."

Nose slid down the rope. Although neither Dog nor anyone else asked why he'd left the hair on the head, he said, "There's no honor in taking scalp of ambusher. Now we go in, have a drink, no?"

I'd never seen a severed head before. It's a whole lot more than, say, someone looking over a tall fence so that only his head is visible. This . . . thing . . . in the mud and slop had no relation to anything human—and yet it did, because I knew this man had been alive not five minutes ago.

I noticed that one eye was closed and the other open in a grotesque wink. The open eye was flat and going gray with no humanity—no life— behind it.

We eased into the saloon, weapons in hand and ready to fire—and found no one. The boozers, the bartender, the whores, the drink-scrounger losers, had apparently hauled ass out the back door, the one that led to the outhouse.

"Shit," Hairy Dog said. "I thought they'd fight."

Big Nose and Jake were behind the bar checking out the bottles. The ones they found to be moonshine with some color added, they flung at the back wall.

"Under the bar, boys," I said. "That's where they keep the prime stock for Powers and his crew."

Big Nose came up with the cashbox, which was hidden away behind a beer barrel. It was a sturdy-looking little safe with one of those numbered dials on the front. "Heavy," Nose said, as he lifted it out and set it on the bar.

"We can take it back to the office an' smash hell outta it 'til it opens," Dog said.

"Yer ass," Jake said. The Derringer appeared in his hand. It took only a single round to spin the box off the bar, its door flapping like the wing of a wounded bird.

There was all paper cash—no coins—in it.

"You see?" Big Nose said. "This is my reward from the gods for hacking that pig-ambusher's head off as he lived."

That seemed to make good sense to Hairy Dog, and the others' faces didn't change in the least—not even Don—so I let it go. Nose grabbed out handfuls of bills and gave a bunch to each of us.

"Damned white of you," Jake said. "I 'preciate it." There was no slur intended; the intrinsic insult was unconscious on Jake's part. I don't doubt that Nose had killed men for less.

We each had several drinks, and we each lit a cigar from the jar behind the bar. They had the flavor of lengths of rope, but they were better than nothing.

The whiskey loosened us up a bit, and we decided to do some target practice. Perhaps sober I'd have done better than I did. I shattered eight bottles of whiskey out of ten—and this was from a draw—so my score wasn't half bad.

Nose and his shotgun blew two and three down at a time because of the spread of the shot in his shells. Dog got all ten of his with one reload of four in his sidearm, but it seemed to me that his draw was a little slow. Jake blew all ten to smithereens. Lucas got nine. Don got a semi-respectable six bottles.

The six of us decided we were hungry and headed for the restaurant. Nose magnanimously waved the procession up and around him. "Now we're friends," he said.

My mouth started running before my mind. "Wasn't Hairy Dog already your friend?"

"Hairy Dog killed my brother. It was a fair fight—left wrists tied together, knives in the right hands—and Dog cut fast and sharp and stabbed when the time was right. Still, Dog knows this, as do I. We travel together. We walk or ride side by side. But not in a new group. You see?"

"Sure," I lied. I had no idea about the philosophy or the rationale behind what Nose had said, but I really didn't much care.

We invaded the restaurant stinking of gunsmoke, booze, cheap cigars, and the usual rank heaviness the unwashed carry around with them.

I handed the wide-eyed waiter a fifty-dollar bill. Since he was making maybe twelve dollars a week—and all the grub he could steal—the fifty was a real big deal.

"I'll pay for everything we eat and drink—that fifty is for you. Some of my friends tend to be a little crude and raucous, OK?"

"What's raucous?"

"This, pretty much: they act like a bunch of wild boar set loose in a fine place to scavenge."

The waiter smiled broadly. "Perhaps we should pull a couple of tables together," he said. "I'll bring some bottles of whiskey—not 'shine—out in a minute."

The cook put on a half dozen steaks, which ordinarily would feed perhaps ten people, and cooked up a damned henhouse of scrambled eggs. He had his helpers mashing enough potatoes to feed damned near an army troop.

There'd been six or eight or so diners in the restaurant when we arrived. Within a few minutes, they were gone and we had the entire dining area to ourselves. I'd told the waiter I'd pay the checks of the folks we frightened away, and that yet furthered their departure.

I can't say that I blamed them. We were a motley-looking crew, and the Indians didn't look like they belonged anywhere but in their caves or wherever they may have lived.

Don's face reddened for some reason, and he appeared suddenly antsy.

"What's the problem?" I asked.

"Well . . . it's this. You've got some real tough boys now. . . ."

"We sure have. But . . ."

"The point is," Don said rapidly, his words almost tripping over one another, "that I need to pull out. My family—my ma an' pa an' everyone—they need me there more than you need me here. I'm . . . I'm really sorry, Pound, but . . ."

"You have nothing at all to be sorry about. I respect a man who takes care of family. When you leaving?"

"I figured, uhh . . . I'm ready to go right now, if that's OK."

"Of course it's OK." I looked at the others. "You boys been listening, so you all know Don is heading out. He's a hell of a man. Let's have a drink to him."

"Hell no," Lucas said. "Let's have *lots* of drinks to him."

Don stood, looked us each in the eye, and walked away from the table. No more words were needed.

The waiter set down a massive bowl of mashed potatoes on our table. Then for no apparent reason, he spun away from the table and dropped, slowly and almost gracefully to the floor. The sound of the rifle didn't reach us until the poor fellow was hit.

All of us hit the floor simultaneously, crawling toward the street windows. Some of Powers's men—we had no idea how many, were firing at us from inside the mercantile, from a freighter loaded with barrels of beer, and other places we weren't aware of yet.

The restaurant street windows were shattered immediately and rifle and pistol fire continued to pepper the front of the restaurant and the wall at the far end.

"Pound," a voice hollered out, "Mr. Powers wants to talk with you!"

Chapter Seven

A man stumbled and weaved out of the mercantile clutching a white ladies' type scarf, waving it back and forth as if he were in a Fourth of July parade and he was carrying the colors.

"Mr. Powers wantsta talk with you, Pound," he said. "He say he don't know no war."

I shouted out, "You tell that pissant that my boys an' me are going to kill the bunch of you—the ones that don't get the hell out of Gila Bend right away. And you tell Powers that I'll be the one who takes him down."

The flag carrier laughed and hawked a mouthful of spit toward us. Hairy Dog put two rounds in his chest. The makeshift flag fluttered to the ground like a wounded bird.

"Dammit, Dog—you can't shoot a man carrying a white flag!" I said.

"Sure I can—I just did," Hairy Dog said.

"Is very big insult to Indian have a man spit at him. That man cannot be allowed to live no longer."

"What the hell, Pound," Lucas said. "We woulda killed him sooner or later anyhow."

"That's not the . . . ahh, shit. Forget it," I said disgustedly.

Jake, Hairy Dog, and Big Nose had led far different lives than I had. The customs, the beliefs, the concern for human life—or the lack of it—were way beyond my scope of understanding, and it made little sense for me to try to figure it out. I recalled sitting in my pa's wagon as he did some trading with a group of nonhostile Indians. On the ground a chubby little kid—maybe two years old—was playing with a puppy, wrestling around with it, holding it while it licked his face. His mother came to him, picked up the pup, cut its throat, and began to skin it out for the stewpot that bubbled a few feet away over a bed of white coals.

I later learned that an Indian would starve to death before he'd eat horsemeat, but any other creatures are fair game—snake, prairie dog, whatever.

Firing from across the street became sporadic—it went from an almost constant barrage to a couple of shots every minute or so. It didn't feel right—not right at all.

I checked my .30-30 to make sure it was fully loaded, jacked another round into the firing chamber, set the rifle aside, and checked the load in my Colt.

"Jake," I said, "I know this goes against your grain, but I have to ask to borrow your Derringer." I wasn't at all sure what I'd need it for—if anything—but it turned out to be providential that I asked for it.

I expected some sort of grief—at least questioning as to why I needed his miniature canon. He surprised me. He flicked his wrist, the weapon appeared in his hand, and he held it out to me. "'Member—there's no safety. The pull is heavy, but watch yourself."

"What's up?" Lucas asked.

"Those sonsabitches have been too quiet over there. Our office is real vulnerable. If they light it on fire we lose our horses, a ton of ammunition, our clothes and gear—everything. Plus, it'd screw us up on a base of operations. I'm going to slide around the back of the buildings and check out the office—see if they've figured out that they can hurt us. If you hear a gunfight, haul ass to the office—but come in the back of the buildings. If I need you, I'll fire three shots with a pause: one—pause—two—pause—three. If you hear that you come on down."

"I want to go down the street in front," Hairy Dog said. "I do not slink around like the coyote—I fight like the mountain cat."

"Look, even if what I think is happening *is* happening, the ones left will have a clear shot at you if you do that. They'll take you down, Dog, and we can't spare you."

"My medicine is . . ."

My nerves were as tight as guitar strings already. I didn't need this craziness. "Forget your goddamn medicine!" I snarled. "I'm running the show here—and if you don't like that, there's the door."

"*El jefe,*" Dog said sarcastically in Spanish—meaning the leader, the chief, the captain.

"In this operation, yes. When we finish it up, if you have a gripe with me, bring it up then."

Dog smiled broadly and took a step toward me. He put his arm over my shoulder. "But I have no gripe . . ." He thunked me soundly on my back with the butt of a fine-looking, bone-handled knife.

"You see?" he said. He turned the knife so that its gleaming blade pointed at me. "Is not a good idea to screw around with Hairy Dog."

I put the snub little barrel of Jake's Derringer in Dog's gut. I'd been holding it since the Indian began his step toward me. "You see?" I grinned. "Is not a good idea to screw around with Pound."

Our eyes locked for a century. Then the edges of Hairy Dog's mouth began to quiver and then rise. Mine did, too. In a moment we were laughing.

"I hope we never come to a death fight, Pound."

"So do I, Dog."

Most of the day was gone, but there was still good light. The wind was whipping about and it had a cruel bite to it, swirling tumbleweeds and bits of paper around in whirlwinds. *Bad night for a fire*, I thought.

I moved very tight to the backs of the stores until I was maybe twenty yards from our office. My guess had been correct: a dozen or so outlaws had their horses ground-tied fifty or so feet away from our enclosure and horses, but of course the horses were calling out challenges to one another—posturing, I've heard it called.

The outlaws had taken wood from the front of the office and placed it along the rear exterior wall. They were drunk and staggering, laughing crazily, having a fine ol' time. I don't know how they planned to start the fire, but with this wind, if it started at all it'd be a real heller.

Two more outlaws rode up, one with a blazing torch, the flames of which were scaring hell out of his horse. The other carried a five-gallon can of kerosene lamp oil. He dismounted first and stood there laughing at the antics of the torchman's horse.

"Well, hell," the torchbearer said, his horse rearing, shaking its head, trying to get out from under the fire that seemed to be attacking him. The man kicked his feet out of the stirrups, drew his pistol, put the barrel deeply into his horse's ear, and fired, stepping away from the animal as it went down.

The other outlaws found that little show hilarious.

I set my rifle aside. I wanted something that would put a major rupture in the kerosene can. I had no idea what degree of accuracy Jake's Derringer possessed, but it certainly wasn't for long-range shooting.

There was not much cover between me and the outlaws. There was a privy that was fairly close, but I'd be in the open as I ran to it.

It wasn't as if it was a long shot to that kerosene. Using my Colt or the .30-30 it'd be about as difficult as shooting at the sky. I simply didn't know what would happen when one of those mammoth rounds from the Derringer was released. The gamblers carry the damned things 'cause they rarely need to shoot more than a few feet to settle an argument.

I gathered up my rifle, the Derringer in my right hand, and made a run for the privy. The outlaws were drunk, and they were far more interested in their colleagues coming to them with the torch and fuel to pay much attention to anything else.

Maybe there is a God up there.

The man carrying the kerosene tripped and fell, and the torchman, drunk enough for any two people, fell on top of the fellow carrying the tin container. I fired my first shot at the kerosene, and as it turned out, it was all I needed—and it's possible I didn't even need that. The Derringer tore most of the bottom out of the container, and the torch was ready and waiting.

There was an orange-blue explosion that rose instantaneously into the sky. There wasn't much sound involved—it was as if the kerosene didn't have energy it cared to expend in a big blast of sound; instead it used its power to scatter bits and pieces of flaming tin all around itself, and straight up, as well.

Once I talked for some time with a gent who fought for the Union. He had but one arm; the other he left at Antioch. He told me what both sides feared most was that goddamned shrapnel. If a Reb took you down with a rifle, well, that's what war is all about. The Reb aimed the rifle and fired. With canister shot from the canons, one of the goddamn things may hit way over there and tear off an arm or a leg—or just plain kill you— way over here.

That's where his arm went, he said, but it wasn't the canister that took his right arm from his body, it was the army surgeon who gave the soldier a pretty good slug of whiskey for an anesthetic and then sawed—with a wood saw like we've all used—the rest off and wrapped up the stump. The fellow told me that there was a pile of arms and legs behind the surgery tent that stood taller than two men atop each other.

The torchman and the fuel carrier flared up like candles, screaming as they died. Slices of tin took out three—maybe four—outlaws. A couple of them looked around for something to shoot at, but I ducked out of sight, next to the privy. The bunch who were left thought it was a real fine idea to get the hell out of there—which is what they did.

I fired three shots into the sky with the pauses we'd discussed, and in a matter of a few moments Hairy Dog, Big Nose, Lucas, and Jake appeared at the back door. I handed Jake's Derringer back to him. "Thanks," I said. "That huge slug purely tore the bottom off a can of kerosene oil."

Apparently, the outlaws hadn't yet invaded the office. Maybe they wanted to get the fire going first, or maybe Billy Powers told them to do it that way for no reason I could fathom. At any rate, everything was as we'd left it. We went back inside. It was as cold as a crypt, and Lucas edged out the front door to grab some wood. There was a single shot from across the street—the flat, powerful sound of a rifle as opposed to the *crack* a pistol makes.

Nothing happened for a moment.

"I guess they didn't get . . ." Jake began to say, when there was a second round from a rifle fired. Split wood clattered against itself as it fell, and then there was a heavier, dull thud. Jake and Dog covered me and Nose as we went out the door. Lucas was twisted over a large armload of wood. He wasn't moving. Blood streamed down the side of his face and there was that horrible sound that a sucking chest wound makes.

"Let's get him inside," I said.

"Yes. We cannot leave this good man to die in the street." A bullet slammed into the door a foot from Big Nose. He ignored it, grabbing Lucas under the arms. I got his legs as a couple more shots were fired at us.

"They will pay for this, Pound."

"Damned right they will," I said.

Dog and Jake brought wood in under fire. The outlaws were either too drunk or too poor marksmen to hit us—except for the one who put two slugs into Lucas, either of which would have killed him. The combination of the head wound and the punctured lung didn't give him a chance.

Lucas was dead before we got him to the floor inside.

"We need to get him back to his people—I don't want him planted on Boot Hill. He's too good a man for that," I said.

Dog thought that over. "Is right. Two of us get a wagon tomorrow, two stay here to cover the office."

"Yeah. And I know just where to get the wagon," I said.

There's always a strangeness to death. Bodies certainly look different when their spirit—or life, or whatever you care to call it—leaves them. The same went for Lucas. That body stretched out on the floor wasn't my friend Lucas—it was a husk, a shell that used to contain Lucas and now no longer did. I stood over him, staring down at his face and the small fire ignited in my gut and began to turn into a large blaze.

The next morning before sunrise, Hairy Dog and I walked down the back of the buildings almost to the end of the block, where the furniture maker, mortician, and funeral guy had his shop. His wagon was outside and the sleek black horse he used to pull the wagon was in a shelter similar to the one at our office. We didn't bother to attempt to be quiet as we hitched up the horse; the funeral fellow must have been a sound sleeper.

When Hairy Dog kicked in the back door, that woke him in a hurry. Dog stood aside the door leading from the room inside where we were. The mortician thudded down the stairs with a pistol in his hand. Dog stepped behind him holding a knife to his throat. "Let's tie the old bastard. He's liable to go running to Powers," I said.

"And gag him, too." Dog plucked the pistol out of the man's hand and in a manner of minutes we had him tied and gagged.

"We'll bring your horse and wagon back," I said. "The coffin will be your donation to a quiet, law-abiding Gila Bend."

We were in an entire room of the goddamn things. Some were finished and polished; others were little more than elongated packing crates with rough wood and piss-poor carpentry work on them.

I walked over to a nice one—polished to a high gleam, with brass handles on the sides. "What do you think about this one, Dog?" I asked.

"Is good." We went to opposite sides and carried the coffin as if we were pallbearers out to the wagon. We slid it into interior of the funeral wagon and drove it back to the office. The horse was very nicely trained, I noticed.

Lucas had gotten stiffer during the night and there was that ugly, raw-meat aura around him that seems to be part of death. Big Nose and Jake helped us load Lucas into the coffin, but we didn't nail the top shut, figuring his ma or pa might want to see him before he was put into the ground.

I knew approximately where his home was, so I drove. A .30-30 stood next to me; Dog had his across his lap. The mud and slush had turned to ice as the temperature dropped over the past few days. That made for a bumpy, often jarring ride, but it beat getting stuck up to the hubs in slop.

After a couple of hours or so, we came upon a young boy with a fishing pole over his shoulder. "Where's the place of the whiskey makers' family, boy? The Murfins?" I asked.

"Ain't no one makes whiskey 'round here, sir."

"Cut the shit, kid," I said. "I don't have the time or the patience for it just now. Where is it?"

The kid swallowed hard. "You see that hill yonder? You go up it an' then down an' right there is the big house. The still ain't there, though."

"Fine," I said. "Thanks." I gave him a dollar, which he was overjoyed to receive. "There's a bamboo fishin' pole in the Sears Catalog that I can buy now!" he said excitedly.

I jigged the horse and we left the kid standing there gaping at that dollar bill as if it had the secret of eternal life printed on it.

We topped the rise and started down, me holding the horse back so the wagon wouldn't overrun him.

"You feel it, Pound?" Dog said.

"Yeah. Somebody's watching us, probably through the sights of a rifle."

As we drew closer to the house, two men, one on each side of the path, stepped out of the scrub with rifles at the ready across their chests. One was an old gent, probably sixty or so. The other was maybe twenty-five.

"What's your business here?" the older man asked.

"My name is Pound. I'm the sheriff over in Gila Bend, at least for the time being. Lucas came to join on with me several months back."

A smile cracked his face. "You'd be fellow who shot hell outta the two turds who gunned Evan's dog, then."

"That'd be me."

"Well then, come on down and break bread with us—your Injun friend, too."

"I'm afraid we're here with bad news, sir," I said. "Real bad news. We have Lucas in a casket in the wagon. He was shot down by Billy Powers's men."

The old man shook his head sadly. "Lucas was my son-in-law, but I loved him like a son. I told him not to go, but he was set an' determined, an' there was no stopping him."

The young fellow came closer to stand next to his pa, tears streaming down his face. "This here's Lucas's brother," the old guy said. "They was right close."

There was nothing to say, so I kept my silence.

"C'mon down to the house—your Injun friend, too, if he was pals with our Lucas. Just give me a few minutes to go ahead and tell my missus. She . . . she's the one who looks after the baby, just like she was her own." He paused for a moment. "Uhh—is my boy boxed?"

"Yessir," I said, "in the best coffin in Gila Bend."

"I'll ask you boys to put him in the barn, outta the sun. Is the coffin sealed up?"

"Nossir. We figured you might want to see him one more time. He isn't torn up too bad."

"Good. Thanks. You attend to that while I talk to my wife." He turned away and walked toward the house, rifle over his shoulder, Lucas's brother stepping with him.

We drove around the rear of the barn and unloaded the coffin. "The father did not cry," Hairy Dog said. "He is a strong man."

We hefted the box in the shady part of the area where the baled hay was neatly stacked. As we were doing that we heard a screech from the house, a long, pained, lament that seemed to go on for a very long time.

"My people sing over their dead. This is not so different."

We gave the horse a bucket of water and walked to the house. Mr. Murfin stood on the porch with what appeared to be a long, wrapped parcel in his hands. As we drew closer we saw that whatever it was, was wrapped in nicely tanned and oiled leather. We stopped in front of the man.

"Is it known specifically which of Powers's men killed my boy?" he asked.

"Nossir."

He sighed. "Well, I guess it really don't matter." He carefully removed the leather from what he was holding. When that was accomplished, he held a Henry Repeating rifle in his hands. The rifle looked like it'd never been used.

I couldn't help myself before I said, "Good God—a Henry lever-action!"

"That it is," the old man said. "They say a man can squeeze off twenty-eight rounds per minute with this weapon. I think maybe you could do a little better, Mr. Pound. She's a .44 caliber and jus' right for the work you're doing. There's a case of ammo out in the barn. I want you to take that, too. It's brass rim-fire—you won't get a dud in a thousand rounds."

He held the Henry out to me as reverently as if he were handing me a baby.

"I can't take . . ." I began.

The old fellow's voice became stern. "You'll take it and you'll use it and you'll rip holes in a good number of those killers in Gila Bend."

The Henry was a beautiful thing, with a cherry wood stock and perfectly blued barrel. It was a tube-loader, which meant that live cartridges were inserted into the tube and the tube into the rifle and locked in. One big advantage to that is a man could load up a couple of tubes and set them aside, and reload with a fresh thirty-six shots in a matter of a couple of seconds. The weapon smelled of gun oil and fine leather. I worked the lever and it clicked quietly, much like a fine clock.

"I thank you, sir," I said.

"Use it well," he said. "It was going to be Lucas's gift when his first son was birthed. 'Course, Rose of Sharon up an' ran off leavin' Lucas and the baby behind."

Hairy Dog had picked up the tanned leather and we rewrapped the rifle.

"Lookit, fellas," Lucas's father-in-law said, "my women ain't in no shape to make up some coffee. Maybe it'd be best if you got in that funeral wagon and rode on. Sorry."

"No need to be sorry," I said. "We need to get back to town."

"The ammo is in the tack room," he said. "Pick yourself a couple of jugs of the finest whiskey you'll ever taste, while you're in there."

"Yessir. And thank you again."

He turned and went into his home. We could just barely hear a woman sobbing. As we were turning the wagon about, Don rode down the hill. His face was grim. He knew that funeral wagon wasn't there to spread good tidings.

"Lucas?"

"Yeah."

"He was one hell of a good man," Don said.

"That he was," I said.

"I'd better get to the house, boys. Take them sonsabitches down for us, will you?"

Hairy Dog nodded.

"You can bet on it," I said.

We drove out a couple of miles or so from the Murfin enclave with little talk.

Eventually, the Indian said, "It is strange."

"What's strange?"

"The women. In my tribe, if a warrior is killed, the women cut themselves and tear their hair out."

"Does that bring the warrior back?"

"Shows respect."

"So whites don't show love or respect, huh? We . . . ahh, screw it. Want a drink?"

"To Lucas."

"To Lucas," I repeated.

I fetched a jug from the rear of the wagon, and we each had a suck at it.

"Our army grows smaller," Dog said.

"I'll tell you what, Hairy Dog," I said, "the men we have now—you, Jake, Big Nose, and me—will kick those drunken clowns outta Gila Bend—or kill them."

Dog grunted his agreement, and we rode along for a bit.

"That's a fine rifle," Dog said. "I hear they're sighted in at the factory. I trust a factory as much as I trust a faro player in a bar."

"Yeah, but the Henry company . . ."

"I think you should test the rifle just to make sure, Pound."

I laughed. "You just want a crack at this baby after I run a few rounds through it. Right?"

"It's a gun I hear a whole lot about. I don't want one, but I want to see what it can do."

"We can tie up over there, by the desert pines. A Henry makes a hell of a racket, and I don't know what this horse is used to."

That's what we did. As I loaded the Henry's tube I could feel the patina of Hoppe's gun oil on it. The tube clicked into place.

"You see a good target, Dog?"

He nodded. "You see that rock with the mica glint by the two cactuses?"

"Sure," I lied. I couldn't see the cacti, much less the rock. "But let's start close and work our way to distance. We've got a case of ammunition."

"There," Hairy Dog said, "that prairie dog is standing up watching us. He's maybe forty or fifty yards."

A lot more prairie dogs would stay alive if they didn't stand up on their hind legs and haunches, as still as cigar-store Injuns. Nosey little bastards—that's their problem.

I took aim from a standing position and severed the prairie dog's head.

"You aim for headshot?"

"I sure did."

I fired a dozen or more rounds at miscellaneous things: rocks, cacti, whatever. I didn't miss a shot. I felt the barrel. It was warm but not hot. I reloaded the tube and clicked it back in place. I handed the rifle to Hairy Dog. He held it to his shoulder and worked the lever action repeatedly, spewing unfired cartridges like rain around him.

"Is good," he said. "At one time a Winchester .30-06 lever action jammed up on me when I was in a bad spot."

"What'd you do?"

"Used sumbitch as a club. Worked good."

We rode for another hour or so with little or no talking. Then, out of nowhere, Hairy Dog said, "We make a deal, Pound?"

"I don't . . ."

"Money makes no importance to me. It's paper. This Henry rifle has meaning. I want it. We trade one thousand dollars for the rifle, right?"

"It isn't worth anywhere near a thousand dollars. You could take your money and buy . . ."

"This is the one I want," he said. "It speaks to me, is a partner."

I had no particular use for a Henry, but it was a gift from a dead friend's relative. The thousand dollars didn't mean any more to me than it did to Hairy Dog. But still . . .

"I dunno, Dog," I said.

Dog smiled. "It is because the old man gave it to you, no?"

"Well . . . yeah."

"Will you ever lay eyes on him again?"

"Probably not." I thought for a moment. "No."

"So we make a trade like your leaders make with my people. I give up the thousand dollars and you give up something that's not worth near that value."

Dog's logic was good.

"OK," I said.

Hairy Dog pulled a knife from his boot. I flinched, but he used it to slice a cut into his right index finer. He let his blood in a tiny stream flow onto the cherry wood stock of the rifle.

"The rifle is mine now," he said. "We are parts of one another."

Dog moved a few steps from me and began firing. He hit a piece of rock about the size of an egg, and skipped and chased it around the prairie. It was an impressive piece of shooting. He fired at something in the distance I couldn't even see but apparently he scored well, judging from the smile on his face.

When the hammer clicked on the empty firing chamber, Dog felt the barrel. "Not hot," he said quietly, probably to himself rather than to me.

"The mercantile should have a Hoppe's cleaning set," I said. "Even with good ammunition, crud builds up in the barrel. You need to keep the rifle clean and oiled."

Hairy Dog laughed. "You sound like my mother warning me to clean inside my ears, Pound," he said. "But you're right. I will buy."

It seemed that Dog couldn't put that rifle aside. He reloaded and fired every so often, blowing a hole in a prairie dog, shooting the head off a short rattlesnake, and puncturing any number of cacti as we drove along.

"Now the rifle is a virgin, ya know? All I shoot with her is nonsense: snakes and cactuses and prairie dogs. What this Henry needs to make it complete is human blood, a human life."

"I don't suppose it'll be real long before you get to do that. The way things are heating up with Powers, we'll need you cranking that rifle."

"Is true," Dog said. "Want a drink?"

"Sure."

Hairy Dog eased himself into the rear of the wagon—still holding his rifle—and returned to his shotgun seat next to me with a jug. We each had a few swallows. Dog replaced the cork and set the jug down on the floor in front of us.

"I been kind of wondering," I said. "What tribe are you and Big Nose from. None of your ornaments are the same, and you speak mostly in English to each other."

"We are brother/friends, but we arose from different tribes. I was born of a woman of the tribe of Tatanka Iyotaka—Sitting Bull, who was the great chief of the Sioux and led the attack that put Yellow Hair in the ground."

"Yellow . . . ? Oh. Custer, right?"

"Yes."

Hairy Dog avoided my eyes as he spoke. "The thing is, I am not a full member of the Sioux. My father . . . well, he was unknown. He was, of course, an Indian—look at my skin and face. Some say he raped my mother. Others say she was willing." He sighed. "Who knows? But all my hair and being a bastard made a difficult childhood for me." He smiled. "I learned to fight—and fight good—very early."

"Big Nose is a full Sioux?"

Dog nodded.

We were silent for a time, Dog caressing his rifle, me driving without paying any attention to what I was doing. We were following a dirt road to Gila Bend, and the horse had no reason to veer off into the scrub. We were forced over to the side by a large freighter pulled by four huge horses, probably with a good deal of Clydesdale blood in them. That set me to thinking.

"Most of our action with Powers has been in the saloons," I said. "If we can get rid of the gin mills, or at least some of them, we'll have an advantage. Some of those losers will drift on, and the ones who stay won't be happy. After all, getting rid of a couple saloons will cut into their profits."

"Is true. You talk of fire?"

"No, there are always men in those joints and even if we tossed torches on the roof and inside, they'd put it out soon enough."

"What, then?"

"I dunno. I'm thinking on it, though."

It'd begun to snow lightly, and the wind picked up slightly as we came in sight of Gila Bend.

I drove the wagon to the rear of the mortician's place, unhitched the horse, and rubbed him down. I was about finished doing that when the owner came out red-faced and angry.

"That's stealin', Pound. You're a lawman right? Lawmen ain't supposed to steal. I'm going to write a letter . . ."

"Shut your yap, or I'll kick your ass around the block," I explained.

He sputtered a bit, but went back inside. Dog started to walk to the alley between the buildings, but I stopped him. "Let's take the back way, behind the buildings," I said.

We did so. As we walked along, I noticed that about ninety percent of the structures had false fronts—areas built up from the roof to give the appearance of another story to the building.

Apparently, before Powers and his men moved in, Gila Bend was a silver town on the grow—or at least the semblance of one.

There was a privy behind several of the buildings, and each saloon had one. The ones behind the bars smelled like the pits were limed perhaps once a century, if that.

I was more interested in the foundations of the gin mills than the privies or anything else. Maybe "foundation" isn't the right word, though. Each building—saloons included—was built from a plate on the dirt ground. Those that had wooden floors nailed them directly to the plate and then built upward from there. The owners who opted for a dirt floor simply built upward.

Hairy Dog had been walking behind me, the Henry held across his chest. Finally, he could no longer contain his curiosity. "What're you looking for?" he asked.

"I'm not completely sure at this point. But c'mon, let's take an alley. It stinks back here."

We went to the office, snow and ice squeaking under our boots. Jake was behind my desk, reading yet another dime novel, this one entitled, *Danger on the Frontier—or—Daniel Boone Saves the West.* "Any problems?" I asked.

"Been quiet," Jake said. "Calvin, the bar-rag, came by scroungin' for change. I give him a nickel. That's about it."

"Gee, a whole nickel," I said. "You're a real sport, Jake."

"Well, hell" he grumbled. "Since you've got us

payin' for our own drinks, I'm goin' broke. I want to collect my thousand dollars an' haul ass outta this town."

Big Nose nodded and grunted.

Dog showed off his Henry to a highly appreciative pair of his colleagues.

"Jake," I said, "how about letting me use the desk for a bit? I have some figuring to do." Jake moved closer to the stove, sitting on the floor.

I pulled down some Wanted posters and turned them over to their blank sides. I settled in behind my desk. I drew some rectangles and lines and so forth, but knew little more than when I'd started. I tried again, said, "The hell with this," and crumpled the posters into a ball and tossed them into our trash can.

"Problem?" Big Nose asked.

"I'm not real sure," I said. "I've got an idea, but I'm not at all sure how it'd work out. It could be important or we could make ourselves look like four bumbling idiots."

Jake looked up from his reading. "I'd jus' as soon look like a bumblin' idiot as set here doin' nothin' about the job of work we're s'posed to be doin'.'"

"Good point," I said. "Just give me a little time to get my information together."

"Information?" Hairy Dog asked incredulously. "My Henry wants to talk an' you want information. It jus' don't figure."

"How about this?" I said. "You three boys lay into the jugs we brought from the Murfins' place while I go down to the mercantile and kinda poke around."

"Jugs?" Big Nose asked.

"Yeah. Damn," Dog said. "We left 'em in that goddamn funeral wagon. Won't take but a minute for me to fetch 'em."

I left the three of them and walked down to the mercantile. I strolled around the store, picking up and inspecting this and that, buying nothing thus far. Their saddlery was decent—not great, by any means, but no too bad either. I went through the farming supplies where the spools of heavy chain were stored for stump pulling and so forth. For whatever reason, that's where the Stetsons were. I picked out a nice one—kind of tan-brown—and it fit just fine. Of course, Stetson never made a hat that didn't fit just fine. I took it back to the counter and paid for it, then left the store.

Chapter Eight

Temperatures dropped, and not only did they drop, but they stayed down. Fellows who chewed tobacco and were forced to be outside for extended periods of time developed beards of frozen tobacco juice, not a particularly pleasing sight. Old Calvin found as much work as he wanted and was able to stay drunk most of the time on pay from the saloons for breaking the ice in the watering troughs out in front of them. Horses developed long, glittering icicles suspended from their lower jaws when they drank.

Two phrases passed for social conversation in Gila Bend: "Cold nuff for ya?" and "Cold nuff to freeze the balls offa brass monkey."

There was next to nothing for me or my men to do; Powers and his crew stayed in the gin mills and stayed too drunk to cause much trouble.

I spent a good deal of time walking around the outer structures, and the more I did so, the more convinced I became that my plan would work.

I've mentioned before the small nugget of heat that slowly turns into a real conflagration, depending upon the situation I was in. That fire was already glowing.

Very little snow accompanied the cold, but the snow on the ground squeaked under a man's boot or a horse's hoof like a stepped-on mouse.

Hairy Dog had bought a rifle cleaning kit and he disassembled, cleaned, and oiled his Henry at least twice a day—sometimes three of four. Jake and Big Nose played cards for pennies. Cheating, they decided early on, was allowed. If one of them got caught, though, he had to give up the pot.

Late one thickly overcast afternoon of the unrelenting cold, I stood at the office window watching nothing in particular when a four-horse freighter creaked and banged down the street, overloaded with barrels of beer. It pulled down an alley to the rear of the saloon with the piano player.

"You boys ready to do some breaking and entering tonight?" I asked.

"Hell," Dog said, "I'm ready to do *anything*." The others agreed with nods and grunts. It was real clear that keeping these boys caged up was very hard on them—they were used to being on the move at all times, and that's the way they liked it.

"OK," I said, "gather 'round the desk here and I'll show you what I have in mind."

I took out some drawings I'd made after the first attempt and spread them in front of me. I explained everything I'd determined in my many walk-arounds, and I told them how I though it would work—if it worked at all.

There was a stunned, disbelieving silence that lasted for a few seconds, and then the three of them talked at once, slapping me on the back, almost cheering, grins as wide as the Mississippi.

The afternoon that slowly turned to night took damned near forever. As we waited, we sipped whiskey and discussed every possible aspect of what we were about to do. We talked, I think, simply to be talking, trying to goose the time ahead a bit.

The fire in my gut was burning nicely now—strong and hot and churning and demanding action.

About midnight I said, "Ready to have at it?"

My men were already dressed for the cold and had been for some time. My question was purely rhetorical.

The cloud cover had stuck around for the night, which was fine. The darker it was, the more difficult we'd be to see. We went out the back door by the horse enclosure and moved down the backs of buildings until we got to the mercantile. Hairy Dog opened the back door with a solid kick that tore the lock and hasp free and ripped the upper hinge away, too.

It was dark in the store—we could see shapes, but the shapes had no definition. That was fine. I knew exactly where I wanted us to go—the farming supplies. Big Nose filled a pocket with licorice whips as we passed the candy display.

Dog, Big Nose, and Jake gathered around me.

"This stuff is goin' to be right heavy," Jake said.

"We don't have to take it far," I said.

It was indeed heavy—and the four of us almost busted a gut getting it down the block to where we needed it to go. The freighter stood, its horses still in rig, feed bags over their snouts, behind a saloon at the end of the block. Jake had more experience driving a four-horse team of draft horses than any of us, so he took that duty. Nose, Dog, and I went back to the gin mill, from which the piano music tinkled merrily and went to work. It didn't take too long. Then, Hairy Dog positioned himself at the front of the bar with his Henry, ready to cut down any outlaws who tried to get out after things got under way.

Jake drove up and stopped. We made the connections we needed to make. Everything was set. No one had gone in or out of the bar since we began our work in the street. I waved to Jake, and he kicked off the brake and got the huge freighter moving.

The heavy chain that encircled the entire base of the saloon became taut, as did the one attached to the long side of the structure.

Jake got after the horses, slapping the reins over their rumps. To them, this was merely another day of business—Jake got no argument from them.

A horribly high-pitched screech was the first indication that anything was happening. The horses, snorting, leaned into their traces. The entire building began to move toward the street, the tearing wood sounding strangely like a massive fire.

Men raced to the batwings; Dog moved them

back with a few more rounds than he needed to. The saloon continued to move, slowly, like a wounded behemoth. Curses, screams, and shouts inside barely reached us over the ripping and destruction of wood joined to wood.

When the saloon was completely off its foundation, Jake swung the horses hard to his left. With a gigantic creaking roar like ice breaking up on a lake, the entire front of the building was torn off and teetered precariously for a moment. Jake asked the horses for a little more, and they gave it to him. The front—batwings and all—crashed down onto the street.

The lanterns inside had been smashed and dumped, and the fire that started was very hungry—and there was lots of dry wood to feed on.

As that fire grew, the one in my stomach diminished.

I waved my men over to me, and we moved down the street to watch the action. Men and women were running, banging into one another, falling: some of them were a bit singed. A whore saw that her hair was on fire and tore it off her head—a wig that had looked quite natural.

The blaze lit up the night sky beautifully—particularly since there was such heavy cloud cover that no starlight was getting through. Big Nose passed around licorice whips and we stood there munching.

I figured the chance of a retaliation attempt that night was about fifty-fifty.

We headed back to the office, added some wood to the stove, and had a sip of whiskey. "There's a chance they'll try something tonight," I said, "and if not tonight, within the next couple of days. We need a man on the roof at all times and a man awake in the office all the time, too. We'll have to sleep in shifts."

The conflagration that last night had looked so pretty was, in the morning, a grotesque mass of charred and broken wood, and smashed glass. The piano, on its back with its four legs unevenly burned away reminded me of a dead buffalo—they sometimes died that way when they were gunned down, on their backs with all four legs in the air.

We decided, after several days of nothing going on, that we needed to keep up our full-time watches. None of us could see Powers letting go without retaliation anything as flagrant, as egregious as hauling one of his saloons out into the street, tipping it over, and watching it burn

I enjoyed the roof watch, both night and day, regardless off the bitter cold. Not only could I see the entire length of the town, but I could see the rear of the other buildings beyond the jail. It was strangely peaceful.

I got to do some thinking on the roof, which was impossible when I was with any or all three of my troops.

I liked teaching when I first got out of normal school—I really did. I liked the kids, their quick smiles, their willingness to accept and learn what I told them or put on the blackboard.

How I got into the bottle was a fog to me. I knew I stopped at the town bar for a beer most evenings, and then the beer grew to a few beers, augmented by a taste of whiskey. I think I gave up the beer and stayed with hard liquor. That's pretty far as back as my memory goes. A couple of things stood out clearly from the fog: the morning I awakened behind the bar to find myself covered with a foot or more of horseshit and mud, and parents pulling their kids out of school. I deserved to be fired, and I was. I recall swamping out the bar, cleaning the spittoons, wiping up the vomit, for the wage of a couple of drinks. It was right about that time I met Zeb Stone.

Good ol' Zeb: purely as crazy as a shithouse rat, but a man I'd take a bullet for. He gave me back some pride. It's odd how things work out. . . .

As I mentioned, I could see pretty much everything from the roof of our office. Maybe that's why the two riders coming into Gila Bend caught my attention. Both wore Confederate officers' coats—which wasn't at all strange—but the bandoliers of cartridges crossed over their chests were a little odd. Both their saddles had rifle scabbards on each side. Each rider carried a sidearm, but I couldn't tell what they were; the weapons were in military holsters with leather flaps over the guns.

There's a certain degree of inherent intuition involved in living outside the law: decisions about other men need to be made very quickly, because they were often a matter of staying alive or pushing up daisies. My intuition told me that these two weren't disgruntled buffalo hunters, pretty much out of work because of the terrible reduction in the herds of shaggies. What they were was bad news. They pulled up in front of a saloon down the street on the opposite side, tied their horses, and went in.

Later that day, a man I recognized rode past the office. Eddie Halpern was a stagecoach and train robber and hired gun I'd met through Zeb Stone. I hailed him, and he rode over to the office.

"Why, damn," he said jovially, "I ain't seen you in an owl's age, Pound." His face changed quickly. "Say, I was real sad to hear about Zeb getting shot up, Pound. He was a good boy—a *damn* good boy."

"That he was." I waited a moment. "What brings you into this screwed up little town?"

He swung a leg up in front of his saddle horn and took a pipe out of his pocket. He was in the process of lighting it when he looked at me more closely. "That ain't a badge you're wearin', is it, Pound?"

"It's a long story, but I'll swear to this: it has nothing to do with you or my other friends."

"On your ma's grave?"

"On my ma's grave."

Eddie got his pipe burning nicely and puffed dense blue smoke from his mouth.

Again, I asked, "What brings you into town?"

"Shit, Pound." He grinned. "Same thing that brings me 'most everywhere I go: money. Some Reb named Powers is payin' big bucks in a range war or some damned thing. He's lookin' for guns. I guess the men he has ain't worth a tinker's damn."

"He's fighting me, Eddie," I said.

"You? What the hell for?"

"That's part of the long story."

Eddie was still for a moment. Then he said exactly what I knew he'd say: "Who's payin' better?"

"You'd better stick with playing the hand you already have, Eddie," I said.

"You don't trust me?"

"No. I don't—not any more than Zeb did when you wanted to ride with us. I don't hate you. Hell, I don't even dislike you. But I don't trust you."

His eyes squinted a bit, and the last vestige of his smile left his face. "I'm liable to kill you, Pound, with or without what's goin' on here."

I held his eyes. "You'll probably get a chance to try real soon. I guess we'll see then, no?"

Eddie cursed, spun his horse, and dug spurs into the animal far deeper than he needed to. I could have simply picked up my .30-30 from next to me and blown him out of his saddle. Hell, for that matter he was well within pistol range. But I watched him ride to where a few of Powers's crew had assembled in front of their saloon.

Zeb Stone wasn't what you'd call a philosopher, but I've never forgotten something he told me: *Never ride with nobody you don't trust all the way,*

Pound. It's like raisin' up a wolf from a pup and playin'
with him an' takin care of him an' all that. One day
that wolf is going to be what he is and tear your throat
out. Same thing applies to men.

I sat out the last few hours on the roof, checking in all directions, watching the street, looking
for anything that worried me. I didn't have to
look far.

Men had been riding in every so often. I've
seen the type all over the place: hired guns who'd
kill anyone they got paid to kill. I recognized some
of them; most I didn't. All told, maybe six or seven
of these backshooters rode in.

Big Nose came up when he was to take over my
shift. "Things ain't lookin' good," he said.

"You mean because of the guns coming in."

"Yeah. I recognized a couple, maybe three of
them. They're not drunken clowns, Pound, like
Powers's crew. Those boys know how to fight."

"So do we, Nose. So do we. And I can't say I'm
real surprised at Powers bringing in fighting men.
He knows that the four of us would go through
his band of stumblebums like a knife through soft
butter."

"I've been wonderin' a bit about that and so has
Hairy Dog—why the hell they didn't attack us
right after we played with their saloon. We figured there's a couple reasons: they ain't got the
balls, an' their little city of Gila Bend is comin'
apart on them."

"Yeah," I agreed. "I wouldn't be surprised if
one or two have been makin' tracks at night,

headed wherever. I doubt there's a single one that'd risk bleedin' for Billy Powers."

Nose nodded.

"I was thinking maybe Dog and I would break into the mercantile again tonight," I said.

"What for?"

I answered his question with a question of my own. "You ever done much with dynamite?"

"Nah. Shit, me an' Dog are kinda leery of that stuff. Some relative of Dog's blew hell outta himself and his family screwin' around with it. Dog said there wasn't enough of the man, his woman, or their four kids left to fill a cigar box."

"I haven't used it either. Maybe Jake has. He's crazy enough to do anything."

"Right," Nose said. " 'Course if he blows us up with it, it ain't doin' us much good."

I couldn't argue with that point.

The wreckage of the saloon we chained and burned hadn't been moved or cleaned away. There was enough room at the near end for even a freighter to drive by, and horseback travel went back and forth with out a problem.

To old Calvin, the official town bar-rag, it'd been as if a large piece of heaven had fallen directly into his world, and gave him full license to pluck its wondrous fruits. It probably would have made a lot more sense for Calvin to gather up whatever unsmashed bottles he could get to and haul them off to a safe place, where he could do his level best to drink himself to death.

Calvin had never been noted as having much, if any, common sense.

So, each morning, red-eyed, staggering, his entire body trembling with a sort of Saint Vitus's dance, he'd scrounge through the burned timbers, smashed tables, and so forth, seeking out his bottle for the day. He'd fall often, but that didn't slow him down. The treasure remained available to him and a few cuts and bruises were of little consequence.

Nose and I were in the office, Jake on the roof, and Hairy Dog out back with the horses.

Nose called me to the window when a pistol report drew a ". . . those lousy sonsabitches . . ." from him. Ol' Calvin was precariously balanced on an upward-leaning beam, looking at the neck of a whiskey bottle he held in his hand.

"Somebody shot the bottle right outta the old fellow's hand," Nose said, voice tight.

"You see that?" Jake hollered down from the roof.

I stood next to Nose at the window, waiting to see what would happen next. What happened was that there was a re-creation of the battle at Gettysburg, with Calvin playing the Rebel forces. Rifle and pistol rounds tore into him, pelted him like a driving rain, putting a faint pink mist in the still air around him. Even after he was dead the firing continued.

We heard Dog's rifle firing off its twenty-eight to thirty rounds per minute the Henry was famous for, and we watched his slugs stitch across the wooden planks of the second story and the glass in the window of the outlaw's quarters. A heartbeat later a man came through the window, rifle still clutched in his hand, a series of crimson splotches across his chest.

There was a barrage of return fire, but Jake was behind the beams we nailed on each side of the roof opening. The way it worked was that the roof man could stand on the ladder we made, and fire at will—unless he put his head up at the wrong time. Nose jumped to one side of the window and I to the other a half second before the glass cascaded inward.

"I guess that about tears it," I said. "We're at war."

"That's what me an' Dog are here for," Big Nose said, his voice as jaunty as a kid's at a birthday party.

Nose watched the window, sweeping the sharp shards away from the bottom sill with his rifle, and I went through the office to the back. Jake stood in the enclosure with his rifle butt at his shoulder, but no target. "We could have a problem here," he said. "A horse makes a helluva big target an' we might need these boys real bad durin' this do-si-do. They could be picked off real easy. I guess my ride is good at the livery 'cause I doubt if the outlaws know which is mine. Nowhere else to put yours an' Dog's an' Nose's though."

"Sure there is," I said. I gathered up the blankets and spare gear from both the cells and took it to the front of the office and dumped it in a pile on the floor. I carried the three feed buckets in and I split a bale of hay three ways and tossed a third in each cell and on the floor of the aisle.

I led each horse in separately, put my buckskin in a cell, Nose's in the next cell, and Hairy Dog's in the aisle. Water wouldn't be a problem. One of the sheriffs out on Boot Hill had used convict labor to dig a well and put in the pump we'd been using, just a few feet from the back door.

"Might get rank in here if the fight goes on for long," I said.

Jake grinned. "Hell, it'll smell better in here than most of the women I've slept with," he said.

I figured Hairy Dog would be the best candidate for going to the mercantile with me. Not only did he have superlative eyesight, but he could move about making no sound whatsoever. I, on the other hand, couldn't see worth a damn, particularly in the dark, and was about as light on my feet as a bull shaggy.

Bursts of gunfire carried on back and forth across the street all afternoon, but it looked like Calvin and the thug Jake shot out of the window were the only two casualties. The saloon the Powers troop was holed up in was on the opposite side of the street, maybe twenty yards down from our office. It was difficult to get off a fully aimed, clean shot because the angle forced the shooter into revealing more of his body than he'd care to—and that applied to Powers's men as much as it did to us.

Although we had a ton of ammunition, we decided it'd make sense not to spray lead, hoping for hit—we'd shoot only when we thought it was possible to bring down the enemy.

Dog I set off long after dark to the mercantile. The night was only marginally lighter than the first foray the bunch of us had made to steal the chain, with a good deal of cloud cover and a slice of moon. We hugged the backs of the buildings, Hairy Dog leading, me a step behind. We'd decided to leave our rifles behind and carry only our handguns, freeing up our hands to carry off what we hoped to find.

When Dog stopped abruptly, I walked directly into him, eliciting a quiet, "Goddamn idjit." We made it the rest of the way to the mercantile without problems.

I half suspected Powers would have a watchdog or two behind the store, but that wasn't the case.

Hairy Dog kicked in the door, leaving a brand new–looking lock and hasp hanging, and we eased inside. We stood still for a full minute, allowing our eyes to adjust to the yet more profound darkness inside the store. I felt Dog bend over and then straighten, and heard an almost silent, angry whispering hiss that brought an image of a coiled and hissing snake to my mind. There was a grunt from across the room and then a thud as something heavy hit the floor.

"Stay right here," Dog said. "Don't move. I gotta fetch my knife outta that fool guard. Hell, he should have taken us down as soon as we were inside."

I waited longer than it should have taken Hairy Dog to come back across the room, my palm sweating against the grip of my Colt.

"Pound," he finally whispered, "I think I found something. Put your hand on my shoulder and follow me."

He led me through the store to what was apparently a separate room. He pulled the door shut, scratched a match, and lit a small candle, since the room was windowless.

"It wasn't locked," he said. "Well," he corrected himself, "it was, but somebody went an' tore off the lock."

Hairy Dog's candle spread precious little light, but it was easy enough to see what the storeowner kept in his private room: stacks of overpriced racy books that showed some tit and a bit of ass and that was about all.

The men in the room before us had, of course, gone through the books, looking for whatever perversions pleased them, and were no doubt disappointed. Hairy Dog called me over to his side. "Lookit this," he said.

The entire large hardcover book was devoted to men spanking women—most often, nude women. The poses were much the same in all the photographs: the woman would be looking over her shoulder with an intense pleading in her eyes, some overly shiny tears running down her face, and her hands clutched together, almost as if in prayer.

Often, the lady's ass showed marks across it, like an abused mule's hide would on his flesh. The price on the book's cover was four dollars. Given the fact that the average silver mine worker made perhaps ten or eleven dollars a week and a cowpoke or ranch hand less than that, I doubted that the storeowner sold many of these things.

"What's the point, Pound?" Hairy Dog asked. "A woman needs to be straightened out ever' so often, I'll admit that, but a whole booka pitchers of it? It's dumb."

"Lookit, Dog," I said, "we don't have time for this shit right now. Gimme the candle."

Dog handed over the candle and said, "There's a role of fuses over there by the ass-whippin' books."

I moved that way. Hairy Dog was correct—it was a roll of dynamite fuses. There was also a spot on the floor that didn't have any dust on it—like something had very recently been removed from it.

"Powers got the dynamite," I said.

"Maybe."

"Maybe, my ass! What else would the mercantile guy stash next to rolled fuses?"

"Damn, if you don't get prickly," Dog pointed out, " 'ticularly to a man who could tear your head off an' shove it up yer ass." After a moment he added, "Only thing we can do is raid the sons-abitches an' get the dynamite back."

The raw stupidity of what Dog had just said irritated me further. "They going to just hand it over, or will they shoot our asses off first?" I asked.

Hairy Dog glared at me, what tiny bit of light there was reflecting in his eyes, which were cold and menacing.

That calmed me down a bit. After a few moments I said, "I think what we need to do is this: We gather up all the 12-gauge shotguns, along with a couple cases of 12-gauge double-ought ammunition. Those fuses are as bright as the magnesium a photographer uses—we'll see them day or night. All we do is shoot at those bright lights and the dynamite will explode in the air."

"I ain't real handy with a shotgun," Dog said. "I never much cared for them."

"You don't *need* to be handy," I said. "That's the beauty of it. The shot pattern opens so wide, it's damned near impossible to miss."

"Be good to know how many of them sticks they got," Dog said.

"Yeah. That's why we need to carry off all the cartridges we can find."

"OK," Dog said. "You wait right here while I fetch up all the shotguns and cartridges I can find and put 'em by the door. You'll bust your silly neck stumblin' around in the dark."

I started to say something but didn't. Hairy Dog was right. I stayed where I was, listening to him moving quietly about the store. When he smashed the glass display case to free up the shotguns, it sounded like an explosion in a glass factory. I was somewhat surprised to find my

Colt in my hand and my finger inside the trigger guard, ready to fire, and I didn't remember drawing at all. It was reflex, I guess. I reholstered the pistol, feeling a tad foolish. I was glad Dog wasn't right there to see how tight I was wound.

Hairy Dog came back and got me, and I followed him again, my hand on his shoulder. It was pitch dark, and how he could see as well as he did amazed me. Even a candle would have drawn Powers's attention to us.

Someone once told me that every Indian has some cat blood running in his veins, giving him the cat's ability to see so well in the dark. It made as much sense as any other explanation I'd ever heard.

We stopped for a moment, and Dog moved something or other around on a counter. Then, he led me to the door, and we loaded our arms with shotguns and ammunition and trekked back to the office with no trouble, in spite of the awkward burdens we muled.

Either Nose or Jake had gotten rid of the accumulated horseshit, which was good, but there wasn't much that could be done about the pungent, ammonia-like reek of the urine except dash buckets of water on it and mop it up.

We put the cases and boxes of cartridges on the floor next to the desk, and the shotguns on top of and around them. Hairy Dog picked up a shotgun, looked at it quickly, and tossed it into the corner near the stove.

"Is 10-gauge," he said. The remaining five were 12-gauge weapons.

Dog went up on the roof to watch, and Jake came down. I explained my plan for dynamite control and the two men were enthusiastic.

"Me an' Dog an' a couple of other boys robbed a plantation one time," Big Nose said. "There was a bunch of old farts shooting at dinner plates a darkie was throwing up and out. Not many plates got busted, I'll tell you that. We got some cash and jewelry."

"Didn't we take a couple horses, too?" Dog called down from the roof.

Big Nose considered for a moment. "No, not from that place. We got the horses a little later. That reminds me of . . ."

It seemed like the Indians were about to launch into a grand tale of their exploits, and we didn't have time for that.

"Goddammit, listen up," I interrupted. "Each of us has to keep a shotgun and a couple pocketfuls of cartridges in hand at all times. Try to blow the dynamite as far out as you can, but if they get close, shoot hell out of them anyway. One stick in here and we're mincemeat—so keep a real good lookout."

"All that's fine, Pound," Jake said, looking over a shotgun. "But when does the fightin' start?"

"Keep your drawers up, Jake," I said. "I know what I'm doing here." *Or, I hope I do anyway.*

"Way I see it," Big Nose said, "they got a bunch of ex-military men over there."

"Deserters," I said.

"No difference, Pound. They will mount an attack, an' they won't wait much longer to do it."

Dog passed around his licorice whips.

"We're ready for 'em," Jake said.

"We are," I said. "We might need more food, though. I'm getting weary of jerky and hardtack."

Big Nose looked over at Dog. "Let's go back to the store an' stock up."

That's exactly what the two Indians did, bringing back a sack of apples, three hams, ten pounds of ground coffee, seven quarts of whiskey, a few large tins of peaches in syrup, as well as tobacco, papers, and cheroots. We all took a turn at one of the bottles, and went to our watches. It seemed like a very long night.

Snow started early the next morning. The storm wasn't like the first of the season—the one where I damned near died—but it wasn't too bad of a replica of it. The wind howled down the street like a malevolent spirit, looking for souls to carry off.

We kept as close a watch as we could on the saloon where the Powers thugs were holed up, but there were so many whiteouts that it was impossible to see clearly. Of course, they had the same problem we had.

I remembered storms from when I was a kid. Sucking at the whiskey facilitated the memories, and I drifted, half asleep, half awake, and let my mind wander.

Pa used to send his cattle dog out in a bitch-storm like this. He'd paid $23.00 for that dog. The seller said the dog was part of the Scottish breed, the collie. It was a joy to watch the dog work the cattle, following my pa's voice and arm commands. He—the dog—would light out after a stray Pa pointed at, and damned near drag it back to the flock. Even when the cattle were moving good, doing what they were supposed to do when moving from one pasture or another, that big ol' shaggy dog was everywhere in the herd: nipping a hock of a slacker, even grabbing the nose of a wanderer to get him going in the right direction. It was something to see.

Pa got caught with his drawers down one day when a storm worked itself into a blizzard and the herd was out in the lower forty acres, about as far away from the barn and their hay and grain as they could get without busting through a fence of two strands of tightly strung barbed wire.

Pa sent that dog out, knowing the animal didn't have a chance in hell of accomplishing anything worthwhile. I guess Pa figured even if a few head made it in, it was better than none. The dog didn't come back, nor did any of the herd out in the lower forty.

I was standing there in the barn sniveling because I knew the dog was either already frozen to death or would be shortly, and Pa cuffed me hard on the back of my head.

"Lookit, Lawrence," he said, "when you bust a hammer or a saw or whatever, do you cry like a sissy about it? Hell, no! You up an' go buy another one. That's what I'll do is get me another dog. All he was, was a tool who shit in my barn an' cost me money to feed."

I remembered this thought very clearly: I thought, "If I had a gun right now I'd kill you, you son of a bitch."

We kept our watches regardless of the fact that the wind-whipped snow allowed only very limited visibility.

I was drinking more than I should and dozing pretty much all the time I was off watch.

I had a pretty heavy booze problem before I partnered up with Zeb Stone—but I'd heard more goddamn Indian hero stories from Big Nose and Hairy Dog than any one man should have to endure.

Jake was slugging the bottle pretty hard, too; his eyes were red rimmed and crusty and I noticed a tremble in his hands that worried me.

Men begin to grind one another when they're confined together too long, even if they're tight friends. We weren't pals—we were four men doing a job: three of us for cash money and one for freedom from the law.

Early in the fourth day of the blizzard, I was dozing, half drunk, when Jake and Hairy Dog hollering at each other woke me up. They were racing beetles that came in with our cut firewood, and there was a conflict about the race: Dog called it a tie and Jake declared his beetle the winner.

"That goddamn beetle shoved mine right at the starting line—hell, you saw it an' you can't say you didn't—and it was still a tie race!"

"Bullshit," Dog exclaimed. "Your *pendajo* beetle is a clumsy pig an' cannot run. This I saw with my own eyes."

The two men had been crouched side by side, and both were rising. I got my feet under me and dove between them, arms extended, taking them down with me.

"C'mon, dammit!" I shouted. "Both of you back off! What's the sense of killing each other when we've got an enemy right across the street to fight?"

"I piss on your enemy, Pound," Dog snarled. "Me an' Big Nose will ride on as soon as the storm ends. We are fighting men, an' racing beetles is not fighting. You stick your money in your ass, no?"

"I'll take the money them two don't want, Pound, an' I'll go across the street right now an' raise some hell," Jake said. "I don't need no goddamn Injuns to . . ."

"Cut it out!" I bellowed. "I can't do anything about the storm, but to leave Gila Bend now—without the money—doesn't make sense."

I thought real fast. I needed these men. I wouldn't have a chance without them. "Look," I said, "suppose we draw straws and the two short ones go across the street and do some spying to figure out if we should attack or if we should hold out a bit longer and wait for them to do something?"

"I am all out of waiting," Hairy Dog said. "My waiting is all used up."

"OK," I said, "how about this: We do the straws like I said. If the two men who cross the street think we should attack, well, we will—tonight. If not, we hold out. Either way, you boys get your money."

There was an uneasy silence in the office. Jake's beetle, after wandering as if confused for a bit, started hauling ass back to where our indoor wood was stacked. Jake stomped on it hard enough to drive it straight down to hell. He held out his hand to Dog. "No more beetles, right?"

Hairy Dog took his hand and the beetle racing crisis was over.

I went out back to pluck four pieces of straw from our broom. I stuck one of the short ones into a horseball and pulled it out with a little glob of horseshit on it, figuring the other men would avoid it. I called Big Nose down from the roof. "You been hearing what's happening from up there?" I asked.

"Pretty much. The plan is good. Let's go up front and draw straws."

The three of my troops—such as they were—gathered around me. I held out my left fist out with all the straw tops even.

We drew cards to see what order we'd choose in. Hairy Dog was first, Jake second, me third, and Big Nose fourth.

Dog looked at the straws for a long moment and then laughed. "You think red men are stupid,

Paul Bagdon

Pound. You think we would not take the straw with the dung. You're wrong." He tugged the short, horseshit topped straw from my fist. "I go." He grinned.

Jake deliberated for a long time for a man who was a shoot-now-ask-questions-later sort. Finally, he chose a straw. It was long. "Damn," he said, and tossed the straw toward our inside stacked wood.

There were only two straws left. I had straight, honest, fifty-to-fifty odds. I don't know that a man can ask much more in any situation. I pulled a straw; it was short.

Big Nose snorted, his face hard and his eyes like embers behind polished black glass. He turned away from us and went back to his roof watch, wordlessly.

"We go, Pound," Hairy Dog said needlessly.

We dressed in our outdoor clothing and covered our mouths and noses with a couple of bandanas each.

"Maybe you know this, but I say it again," Dog said. "No good to run outside, Pound. Is like a fire in the chest. Do everything slow, as if you are a dried up ol' woman."

I'd never come across a man with burned lungs, but I'd seen a few horses. The poor sonsabitches had to work real hard for each breath, they stopped eating, and they croaked, unless someone was kind enough to put them down. No horse—and no man, I guess—gets better from burned lungs. I decided to pay real close attention to what Dog said.

The wind was damned near strong enough to blow a man out of his boots. The cold was a living, malevolent force—a force to be reckoned with. Further, it was a force that couldn't be overcome. I spat; the saliva turned to tiny, glistening bits of ice before it struck the ground.

I stayed a stride behind Dog. He knew where he was going; I didn't.

He stopped. I walked into his back. "Hot damn," he shouted into my ear. "This here's a freighter with six barrels of beer on it. You stand right here like a statue, Pound. I'm gonna roll one'a these babies back to the office."

"But," I shouted, "what we're doing . . ."

Hairy Dog had jumped atop the wagon and shoved a barrel off. It crashed pretty hard but didn't break or leak.

"A man needs a beer now'n again," he yelled, face close to mine. "You stay here." He was gone into the wildly whipping snow, probably with a major grin on his face, using his hands and feet to keep the barrel rolling.

I didn't see that I had a choice, so I stood there stomping my feet and rubbing my arms and hands until I felt Hairy Dog's hand on my shoulder. How that man could see in this weather purely confused me, but he could.

He appeared like a chimera next to me. "I'll go around the building—see what I can see. You wait here."

I started to protest, but he was already gone. Into the maelstrom. I didn't see or hear Dog until he touched my shoulder and led me to a huge pile of cut and stacked wood that cut the wind some, and let us talk.

"Most of the windows are too froze over to see through, but I walked all around the building, looking in where I could. I took down a man, but I doubt that he was a watchdog—I think he jus' stepped out to piss, is what he did.

"The dynamite—two cases of it—is sitting on the bar. There are thirty or so men and eight or ten whores. They're all boozin' pretty hard. Looks like each man has at least a rifle and a pistol and whatever else he might be carryin' concealed."

"Can we take them?" I asked.

Dog grinned. "Yeah, we can. There ain't but six or eight real fightin' men in there—the rest are war crazies, drunks, and saddle tramps Powers signed on."

We got a tiny window of light as the wind shifted. The front of Dog's albino wolf coat was painted with frozen blood, and so were his sleeves and gloves.

I looked closer. "You hurt, Dog? Looks like you're leaking blood. Let's . . ."

"Is no my blood," he said. "The man pissing? I cut off his head and mounted it on a mop handle stuck in the snow." He reached into his pocket and took out a pistol. "Is nice .45," he said. "See the horn grips?"

"Yeah. It's a nice gun, Dog, but . . ."

"But what?"

"Well . . . nothing. Let's get back."

I don't think Indians and whites can speak the same emotional language, or live anywhere near the same life. Hairy Dog had had just killed a man, decapitated him, and mounted the fellow's head on an inverted mop jammed into the snow. The very thought of it made me queasy, made me swallow hot bile that'd risen in my throat. Dog, on the other hand, believed that nothing done to an enemy is too barbaric, too inhuman, too disgusting.

"What?" he asked again.

"Nothing," I said. "Nothing at all."

We crossed the street, barely able to stay on our feet in the wind. Dog waved his rifle over his head so our own boys wouldn't pick us off. I was certain Big Nose would see the signal; I wasn't at all sure about Jake.

Jake let us in and handed us each a bottle. We shucked our outer clothes and damned near climbed right on into the stove.

Big Nose asked Dog, "Can we do this?"

"Yes," Dog said.

Jake stood. "Well, hell, then—let's get to it."

Chapter Nine

I was just about to make a couple of points about how we could attack Powers effectively when Nose kicked open the door, snatched up the shotgun that was standing on its butt next to it, and fired into the sky.

I hadn't seen the fuse burning, probably because I wasn't looking quite that way, but I sure saw the explosion when Big Nose's shot hit the stick. It was the blindingly bright—the purest, hottest white in the world, and then suddenly, it was red-orange. The snow acted as fast-moving reflectors, throwing the colors into the sky.

We all grabbed shotguns—and we didn't have to wait long to use them. The fuses, like I said, hissed as bright and hot as magnesium flares, and we blew the dynamite out of the sky with no more trouble than we'd have shooting pigeons. It's not impossible to miss a near target with a 12-gauge, but it's actually rather difficult. The pattern of shot opens up so wide so fast that a few pellets are almost bound to hit the target. The one problem I had was leading a dynamite stick a bit when one of my boys would blow one in my line of vision. The flash of it exploding would create a gauzy white curtain over my eyes for a moment, and I could no longer see my target.

It was like looking at a mid-August sun for a few moments longer than necessary, and white spots floated for a bit. By the time I was able to refocus on the target, one of the others would have plucked it out of the darkness. My eyes were tearing, and I was glad to see that Dog's and Nose's were, as well.

Jake had the best seat in the house: he was on the roof. He had the benefit of breathing unsullied air and the best vantage point. I was a little surprised to hear him fire his rifle every so often, until I saw a thug flip up into the air a good ten feet, like a rag doll thrown into the sky with a few parts missing— like an arm, a head, and a leg. Jake whooped like a kid at a circus. "Dumb bastid," he shouted.

Later, Jake told us that most of Powers's men were lighting the fuses of their sticks of dynamite behind the cover of their saloon, but every so often some chowderhead would touch off a stick within Jake's view. The shotgun pattern wouldn't carry that far with enough punch to do any damage, but Jake's rifle sure would. When he hit a stick the man purely came apart.

It was coming dark, with snow spattering about now and then. It'd been dusk-dark all day, with a thick cover of gray clouds blocking any of the feeble winter sun.

We'd expected that Powers would eventually

move some of his troops down the street behind the buildings to put them closer to our office. It would make hurling the dynamite easier and perhaps more effective. We were correct. There was an out-of-business apothecary shop kitty-corner across the street, and the men broke in the rear and were tossing dynamite at us from behind the cover of the boarded up storefront.

If one of those sticks of dynamite had made it past our guns, the four of us would be painting the office with our guts, blood, brains, and flesh. The thing is, none of them did. Hairy Dog—and Jake, for that matter—were as happy as seven-year-olds at a birthday party playing a game—and Big Nose was shooting with the efficiency of a regulator clock.

Even with the door wide open and the window adjacent to it shot out, the office was filled with gun smoke and its acrid, eye-burning, fog.

A couple of moments went by that no dynamite was thrown at us. We all rubbed our eyes and held our shotguns at the ready. Still, nothing happened.

"They're outta dynamite," Jake said.

"Nah," Dog said, "there were two cases on the bar. I dunno how many sticks come in one, but they ain't out."

"I say we charge 'em, Pound," Big Nose said. "The way they were wasting explosives shows that they're dumb—that they're not fighters. If we go over there now . . ."

"Jesus, lookit this!" Jake yelled.

Powers and his crew had snagged a small, fancy surrey from the stable, filled it with straw and, no doubt, dynamite—and were pushing it on the street toward our office from an alley about half-way between their saloon and the apothecary.

My personal fire was churning and seething at my gut, demanding that I do something to quench it before it consumed me. My palms were sweating—they always do before a fight. I saw that as a good sign. I was as weary of screwing around with Powers as Jake, Nose, and Dog were.

"It ain't usual," Nose said, "to see anyone do something that goddamn stupid—that cart—in a battle."

Jake clambered down the ladder.

"Yeah," I said. "An' you can just wager it's the crazies and the expendables that're pushing that little surrey—Powers wouldn't risk fighters on such a dumb move."

"Well, look, I don't care to spend the rest of my life screwing around with these clowns. I'm gonna go an' blow that wagon," Jake said.

"C'mon, Jake, if the goddamn thing is loaded with dynamite, you get blown apart. An' if not, the gunmen will trim you down. You ever think of that? That these boys have set up a ploy that'll draw a couple of us to them—and then they'll start shooting?"

"They ain't smart enough."

"You don't know that, Jake. Here's the thing . . ."

"No!" he cut me off. "*Here's* the thing." He held

his rifle over his head and his pistol in his hand. "I'm purely done sniffing around these saddle tramps."

"But . . ."

Jake booted the door open and ran outside. I saw the first couple of slugs hit him because I was right in front of the door. He was spun around by the impact of the bullets, and he fell to his knees. He'd dropped his pistol, but he worked his rifle like someone drawing water from a well, his shots very close together. Another slug hit him in the shoulder, and I guess one in his neck. Blood gushed from his mouth and his nose, but he kept on firing that .30-30.

There was a massive explosion in the street— the whole goddamn surrey came apart, and the men pushing it did, as well. It was spectacular; pieces of flaming wood and men and surrey parts rushed upward volcanically in a blaze of orange- red fire. There seemed to be nothing left of Jake but a dark puddle on the dirt of the street. He'd been a good fifteen feet away from the cart when one of his slugs found the dynamite, and the ex- plosion had taken him in its upward spew.

"Son of a bitch," I said quietly.

Big Nose shook his head from side to side slowly. "Was good man, that Jake," he said. "Crazy but good and strong with the bull's balls. He didn't know fear."

All of us were quiet for a minute or so, watch- ing pieces of char drift down from the sky. Even- tually, Hairy Dog spoke up.

"Pound," he said, "suppose you get taken out? It ain't like it's impossible, ya know? Then Nose an' me been wastin' a bunch of time an' ammunition for nothin, 'cause a dead man can't pay what he owes. It don't seem right."

"Dog speaks the truth," Big Nose said. "If you croak, we don't get paid."

"Yes, you do," I said. "In the middle drawer of the desk is a map I drew up. There's about seventy-five thousand dollars at the place I marked. You boys split it."

"Hell." Dog grinned. "It'd be easier to gun you now."

"Help yourself, Dog," I said. "'Course I could put a round in your head, too, an' Nose and I would split the cash."

The three of us laughed quietly—but it seemed like a nervous laugh, a bit forced.

It struck me that these men were sadistic, hardened killers, thieves, and rapists—as crazy as shithouse rats. Life—their own or that of others—had essentially no meaning to them. I shuddered slightly.

"Now we must attack," Nose said. "If we can kill those in the saloon, our work is finished."

"That's probably where the real fighters are," I said. "And I don't doubt that most of the cowards are spurring their way out of Gila Bend. The odds are getting better. One thing," I said, perhaps louder than I needed to, *"Powers is mine."*

"We remember, Powers is yours," Nose said.

"Be nice, if we could get our paws on somma

that dynamite," Dog said. "We could take 'em from three sides an' blow their asses off."

Big Nose smirked. "It'd be nice if we were *Eoa Lok Tatoa*, the great bear that cannot be killed," he said. "But we're not."

"So, let's figure this out as best we can," I said, "since we don't have explosives and we're not bears. I've been in that saloon a few—more than a few—times." I turned over a Wanted poster and sketched a long rectangle onto it, using a chewed-up nub of a pencil.

"Is there any booze?" Hairy Dog asked.

I was confused—irritated for a moment. "It's a saloon, Dog, not a goddamn church. Of course there . . ."

"*Here*, I mean. Damn, Pound, you're for sure gettin' porky."

I ignored Dog's comment but took our last bottle out of the deep desk drawer and tossed it to him. He pulled the cork with his teeth, hit the bottle pretty hard, and passed it to Big Nose, who sucked it a bit and then handed it to me. I did it justice.

"Now look," I said, pointing at my drawing. "Here's the windows on the sides. Maybe they're boarded up by now. I dunno. Here's the bar—it runs pretty much the whole length of the room."

"Looks easy enough," Nose said. "We jus' bust in the front an' fight. If we live, we win."

"No, wait. Here's a problem. This place has an actual second floor—a couple of rooms for the whores to conduct their business, and at least a couple more, like hotel rooms. You can bet the gunsels Powers brought in aren't about to sleep on the barroom floor like the cannon fodder does. If we come charging in, the boys upstairs can pick us off like birds on a fence."

"Are there windows up there?" Big Nose asked.

"I dunno. I think there were at one time, but I'm pretty sure they've been boarded up. But either way, if we got into a gunfighter's room, we'd bring the whole bunch down on us."

"A knife sliding through a throat makes no sound," Nose said.

I hefted the bottle, took a suck, and passed it around again.

"Even those morons," I said, "know we won today. We lost one man an' they lost . . . what? . . . maybe twenty? I thought they might post extra guards tonight an' then get drunk. The guards . . ."

Hairy Dog held up his hand to shut me up. His voice was flint edged, irritated. "You think Big Nose an' me are white men?" He spit on the floor. His eyes, hot and angry, held mine. "We piss on these guards after we kill them, after we open their throats. We can do this, Pound."

I was sure Dog's claims were valid and true. He and his partner hadn't stayed alive all this time by making blunders in battle. "OK," I said. "You kill the guards. Then what?"

"We go in shooting," Dog said. "Whether they're dunk or sober don't matter much—we're better fighters. The ones upstairs we kill, too. Big Nose, you agree with me?"

Nose nodded. "Yeah," he said.

"OK," I said. "Let's give them some more time to get liquored up and then have at it."

We cleaned our weapons, although they didn't need it—we pretty much cleaned and oiled them daily.

You know how a specific, repeated sound can drive a man loopy? Big Nose was honing his knife with a stone, and with each motion the length of the blade made a *skreeeeeeeech* sound. It wasn't a particularly long knife by West Texas standards— Jim Bowie's best approached two feet—and Nose's blade was a mere eleven inches or so. He honed for maybe an hour and when he tested the blade with his thumb and grunted his satisfaction, I was inwardly jubilant.

Then he slid the knife into his boot and tossed the sharpening stone to Hairy Dog. Dog *screeeeeeeched* for about an hour.

There's a sharpening of all of a man's senses just before a battle: he sees better, more clearly; he hears better; and he moves faster and smoother. In a sense, he comes to believe he's invincible.

There's a scent—an odor—to it, and men who survived Antietam and Gettysburg told me about it. One one-legged Reb I talked to told me that the smell before lightning strikes is what becomes a cloud around fighting men who're ready. He also said—and I believe him—that he walked past an opening in the woods at Cemetery Ridge and a Catholic priest was saying a mass and giving communion, and that the fellow could smell blood and just-slaughtered meat.

I'll never know what possessed Bobby Lee to order that cretin Pickett to do what he did, but if they were both standing in front of me I'd feel not an ounce of compunction in shooting both of them down.

It's always difficult to tell what an Indian is feeling, but I'd wager my good buckskin horse that the two Indians were feeling what I was.

Finally, after a century or so, I stood.

"Ready?"

"I was *born* ready to fight," Hairy Dog said.

"Ready," Big Nose quietly.

Each Indian had a .45 tucked in his belt, a shotgun in his left hand, and a .30-30 held in his right. Each had his boot knife clenched firmly between his teeth.

I carried my holstered .45 as well as another stuck behind my belt. Like Dog and Nose, I had a shotgun in my left hand and a .30-30 in my right.

"What about extra ammunition?" I asked.

Both Indians grinned. "If we need more ammunition," Nose said, "we're going to be too dead to shoot it."

None of us shrugged into our heavy winter coats; they'd have slowed us down.

The plan was this: The Indians would go out through our back door and split, each going in behind the buildings to where they'd cross the street. They'd work their way back to the saloon, eliminate the guards, and call me in by lighting a bunch of matches at once. It was a dark and overcast night; I'd be able to see the signal. When I trotted over, we'd charge right in and start shooting.

"There's one thing," I began to say.

Nose waved a dismissive hand. "Yeah, yeah," he grumbled, "Powers is yours."

"Take some soot and char from the stove an' darken your face," Dog said. "Your pale skin is like waving a flag."

The Indians went out the back and I stood at the front door, watching for their signal. Of course, I thought I saw the matches struck a million times before it actually happened.

My palms were sweating copiously and my gut fire was way the hell out of control. I was ready.

I didn't doubt for half a heartbeat that Big Nose and Hairy Dog would take out whatever number of watchdogs Powers posted, and that they'd do their gory work silently.

When the signal came, it seemed as vivid as a stroke of lightning. I left the office, crossed the street, and hugged buildings and doorways as I made my way to Powers's saloon.

It sounded like a pretty rowdy crowd in the joint as I approached—or else well boozed up. There was lots of braying laughter, squeals from the whores, and general gin-mill racket.

I came upon a guard about seventy-five feet from the saloon. He was on his side, like a child sleeping through a night, with one hand under his head and his body kind of tucked upward.

The wide puddle of blood around his head and upper chest was inky black in the murky, over-cast, moonless night.

I made it to the side of the saloon, and after a moment, I felt a gentle hand on my shoulder. I don't know how Hairy Dog had crept up on me so quietly on the squeaky snow, but he did.

He whispered into my ear, "Nose is on the other side of the door. We meet an' we attack through the front."

The batwings had long since been removed with the coming of winter, replaced by a wide, carved, wooden door that looked like it had come from a church. In fact, it no doubt had—possibly from the burned-out hulk I'd seen as I rode into Gila Bend a bunch of months ago.

Both Indians had put their knives away. Every-thing from then on was going to be gunpowder and bullets.

Big Nose signed to me that the door swung in-ward. He pointed to me and then to himself to the left, and to Hairy Dog to the right. The Indi-ans stood on each side of me, slightly hunched, weapons ready.

I caught each of their eyes for moment, took a long step back, and hit the door like a locomotive plowing into it. Nose and I dove to the left; Dog to the right.

We had no particular targets. We intended to kill everyone in there except the whores. I was certain a couple of them would go down, but that couldn't be helped.

I squeezed off the first round from my shotgun and blew apart a fellow going for his holstered pistol.

The 'tender was reaching under the bar. I used my second round on him. The lamps in the joint were large and cast a good deal of light. Part of my pattern must have caught the lamp over the 'tender: the glass reservoir shattered and a liquid sheet of burning kerosene flowed the wall to the floor, licking off to its sides, as well.

Our shotguns were double-barreled Remingtons and I'd fired twice. That fine weapon was good for nothing just now, beyond a club, so I tossed it aside. I shifted my .30-30 to my left hand and drew my Colt. Nose had fired his first 12-guage round at four men at a table playing cards. The money, cards, bottle, and glasses erupted; the men went down. Those 12-gauges were mean sonsabitches.

I had no idea whether Powers had used all his dynamite in his ineffectual charge, but there wasn't a case of it on the bar where it originally had rested.

A stud on the second floor rushed to the railing with a rifle, no pants, and an admirable erection. I shot him in the face.

A slug gouged a groove in the side of my head. I had no idea where the shooter was, but apparently Hairy Dog did. He put a couple of rounds into the chest of a fellow on the second floor, who made a spectacular dive through the railing after being hit. My Colt was empty; I holstered it and pulled the second one from behind my belt.

Big Nose came rolling across the floor, cranking his .30-30, making damned near every round a killing shot. I had a good look at his face and the observation stayed with me; it showed no more excitement than it would if he were sitting at a campfire, smoking and dreaming. But his eyes—Jesus—they burned, glistened, with the fire of the very hottest corner of hell.

Hairy Dog was a noisy fighter when he was engaged, the direct opposite of his partner. He whooped, laughed, and cursed as he threw lead around the saloon.

The last of Powers's men standing on the first floor was a half-breed Indian with long, greasy braids and knife scars on his face. He dropped his pistol on the floor and raised his arms in surrender. Hairy Dog shot him in the heart.

I never really noticed the racket a gunfight created until it was over. My ears were screaming like buzz saws in my head, and I was dizzy from breathing nothing but gun smoke. Big Nose was dripping sweat, and he'd been hit at least twice—his shoulder was bleeding and so was the calf of his right leg. Dog was rifling the pockets of a dead gambler.

The bar area looked like a painting done by a crazy man: The floor was littered with the dead and dying, and a haze of smoke made everything look hidden behind light gauze. The fire I'd

started with the lamp when I shot-gunned the
bartender was spreading. It'd followed the length
of the bar and was well up into the walls. A cork
was forced out of out of a bottle of booze with a
loud *pop!* and I instinctively drew my Colt. It's a
good thing I did; I hadn't reloaded it. I did so and
holstered it.

"Pound," a voice called from the second floor,
"me an' my boys didn't sign on for this shit. We're
ready to make tracks outta here without no more
killin'"

"How many are you?" I asked, my voice dry
and raspy.

"Was four. You an' your Injuns killed two. Let
us come down an' we'll saddle up an' ride."

"Powers up there?"

"Yeah," Powers answered from behind a door.
"I don't give a good goddamn what happens
to these cowards, but it's gotta be me an' you,
Pound."

"You two hired guns come down the stairs
hands raised and get out of Gila Bend. If I ever
see either of you again, I'll kill you. You make a
move that turns us nervous, we'll kill you right
here."

There was a silence.

"We're comin'."

These fellows looked they'd been ridden hard
and put away wet—shaggy, sweaty, bodies trembling. One had a white cloth—it looked like a
piece of a dress—wrapped around his head.
Blood was seeping through it. The second man's

left arm hung uselessly at his side, blood dripping from his finger tips. When they'd made it to the middle of the stairs Hairy Dog and Big Nose opened up on them. I hadn't seen that coming. I turned to the Indians, about to speak.

Big Nose beat me to it. "We cannot take snakes as prisoners. This was a war. They lost."

"But they would've just ridden the hell out of here! There was no reason to kill them!"

"Sure there was," Hairy Dog said. "If you ever wanted to walk around anywhere without looking over your shoulder, they needed to die." He turned his head and spat on the floor. "They was cowards, Pound."

Blood from the furrow in my head was running rather freely, but not in an amount that I was afraid of. I'd been shot worse. I rubbed some that blood between the thumb and forefinger of my right hand, while I was trying to figure out a response to Dog and Nose.

"Lookit," I said. "Those men were unarmed and wounded. We'd killed their partners. All they were doing was trying to get out of Gila Bend, and you two shot them down. Where the hell's the sense in that?"

"The sense is," Big Nose said, "is them sonsabitches would have killed us in a second if we weren't the fighters we are. Damn, Pound, for an outlaw and gunman, you sure are passing stupid."

"The way a white man fights is . . ."

"I know how white men fight. That's why I've

killed so many of them. Dog and me are finished here. Give us our money and we'll ride."

"Maybe you're finished here," I said, "but I'm not. And until I take down Powers, I won't be done."

Powers had quite obviously been listening to our conversation. "Pound," he called down. "You come on up here an' we'll have a good ol' fashioned gunfight. You got the balls for that?"

"I'll go one better than that," I said. "I'll give you my words these two Indians will let you walk by them an' out the door if you're as fast and as good as you say you are."

"Your word don't mean shit to me, Pound."

"It does to the Indians, and that's what counts."

Powers seemed to think it over a bit. "Yeah, OK," he said. "I can't see that I got nothin' to lose."

"Go down to the end of the hall, and I'll come up the stairs to face you. Fair enough?"

"Fair don't mean a goddamn thing more than your word does, but come on."

Except the occasional moan of a man on the floor dying, it was as silent as a cemetery at midnight in the saloon. The fire from the wall and ceiling was moving right along to the second story, but other than some crackling and the snap of dry wood catching fire, it made little sound.

My hands were hot and sweaty and my gut-fire promised to burn right through me if I didn't get a move on and get this thing finished, one way or another. Powers moved to the far end of the hall, and I came to the top of the stairs. He'd left the door of the room he was in open when he came out of it. There was an open wooden case of dynamite against the wall.

He took his position, the standard gunfighter stance: slightly crouched, left boot back maybe a foot, body angled slightly. His right hand hung just barely above the grips of the .45 in his holster. There was a smirk on his face, the kind one sees on smartass kids who sass their teachers.

I topped the stairs, backed a bit, and set myself up.

Things get slow in a one-to-one battle to the death like this: movement and motion were lagging the slightest bit. Why that is I don't know. But I've talked to gunmen who've told me the same thing.

Powers didn't attempt any eye games with me. Our eyes locked and stayed that way. He flicked his left shoulder a bit to see if I'd react; I didn't. It was his right shoulder, arm, and hand I was concerned with.

The fire had licked its way to the second-floor ceiling, and I could feel the heat emanating from it. I didn't think about it; I didn't think about anything but the Colt .45 in Billy Powers's holster.

There was a patina of sweat on Powers's forehead, but I didn't know whether it was from nerves or the fire moving closer to him. A fat drop hung from his eyebrow for a moment, then dropped down into his eye. That's when I drew. With that slowing effect—whatever the hell it was—it seemed I had a better part of a day to draw and fire.

Powers's pistol had barely cleared leather when my first two slugs took him square in his chest. I kept firing; a couple more rounds went to his gut and two to his head.

There was no question whatsoever. Billy Powers was dead, along with his army, his Confederate sympathies, and his disregard for life.

The ceiling fire was moving faster now, hungrier for fresh fuel. I ran back down the stairs, empty Colt still in my hand, hollering, "Come on, boys—we gotta get outta here! That goddamn dynamite is gonna go!"

Dog and Nose didn't question me—they hauled ass to the door, with me a couple of feet behind them. We ran a good ways down the street and then stood there in the arctic cold, sweating, waiting.

After perhaps five minutes dragged past, Big Nose shook his head. "Is no dynamite . . ." he began.

Just then the entire saloon rose a good foot from the ground and was wrenched apart as if a twister hit it. The sound was monumental, and it seemed to go on long after the destruction of the building had been wrought.

The explosion lit the whole town of Gila Bend, pushing aside the darkness, burning through the cloud cover.

"You done real good with Powers," Hairy Dog said.

"Right now," I said, "I'd rather do real good with that bottle back at the office. This shit takes something out of a man."

Big Nose shook his head slowly. "No, Pound—you're wrong. It puts something *into* a man."

We turned our backs on the fire and squeaked down the snowy street to the office.

A couple months later I saw the judge's surrey parked in front of the hotel. There were lots of people on the street, laughing, talking, carrying on like they would in any West Texas town. It was good to see that. A kid and a dog ran past me—best friends, no doubt.

I went into the restaurant bar and sat down at the judge's table.

"I have to admit," he said, "that I didn't expect a bloodbath such as you created, Pound, nor did I anticipate you burning down parts of Gila Bend that could have been put to better uses."

"A deal's a deal," I said. "You didn't mention any stipulations or so forth when we talked before."

He smiled and put his hand out to me. "To tell you the truth, I was relatively certain Powers would kill you within the first few days."

"He didn't."

"Obviously." He poured cognac into a glass and pushed it across the table to me. "It looks like our business is complete, Pound. You're a heck of a lawman—unorthodox, but you get the job done." He sipped at his cognac. "I'll need the badge," he said.

I started to unpin it, then stopped. "No. I want to stay on as the sheriff of Gila Bend." I hadn't made that decision a hundred percent before, but now, facing the judge, I realized it was what I wanted.

"I'm not sure I can . . ."

"Cut the horseshit, Judge. You haven't lied to me before, and there's no reason to start now."

He leaned back in his chair. "The pay is barely what you'd earn as a cowpoke," he said. "The town won't even pay to plant you should you be killed, Pound."

"I don't plan on being killed. And the money means nothing to me."

The judge refilled both our glasses. "I guess we have a deal then—Sheriff."

"Not quite," I said. "I've hired on a couple of deputies."

"The budget doesn't allow . . ."

"I'll take care of their pay, and they each have a couple of thousand behind them right now—cash money."

"Who are these two?"

"A couple of Indians who are the best men in a fight I've ever seen."

"Indians? I can't . . ."

I unpinned my badge and tossed it on the table in front of the judge.

"Jesus God, boy, but you're a pain in the ass. You don't know anything more about negotiating than a prairie dog does." He picked up the badge and handed it back to me.

"Deal," he said, holding out his hand again.

"Deal," I said, taking his hand and shaking to seal things up.

Cotton Smith

"Cotton Smith turns in a terrific story every time."
—*Roundup Magazine*

Tanneman Rose was a Texas Ranger turned bad. When he and his gang robbed a bank, he brought shame to the badge. A jury found him guilty, a judge sentenced him, but Rose swore he wouldn't die in prison. Instead he died while trying to escape. Time Carlow helped to capture his fellow Ranger that day at the bank, and now he's investigating a very odd series of murders. Each victim was involved in sending Tanneman Rose to jail. Could it be a coincidence? Or is Rose's gang out for revenge? Or Rose, himself? Time doesn't believe in ghosts—or coincidences. He's got to find the answers and stop the murders…before he becomes the latest victim.

DEATH MASK

ISBN 13: 978-0-8439-6200-0

COVERING THE OLD WEST
FROM COVER TO COVER.

Since 1953 we have been helping preserve the American West
with great original photos, true stories, new facts,
old facts and current events.

True West Magazine
We Make the Old West Addictive.

❏ **YES!**

Sign me up for the Leisure Western Book Club and send my FREE BOOKS! If I choose to stay in the club, I will pay only $14.00* each month, a savings of $9.96!

NAME: _____

ADDRESS: _____

TELEPHONE: _____

EMAIL: _____

❏ I want to pay by credit card.

❏ **VISA**   ❏ **MasterCard.**   ❏ **DISCOVER**

ACCOUNT #: _____

EXPIRATION DATE: _____

SIGNATURE: _____

Mail this page along with $2.00 shipping and handling to:
**Leisure Western Book Club
PO Box 6640
Wayne, PA 19087**
Or fax (must include credit card information) to:
610-995-9274
You can also sign up online at **www.dorchesterpub.com**.
*Plus $2.00 for shipping. Offer open to residents of the U.S. and Canada only.
Canadian residents please call 1-800-481-9191 for pricing information.
If under 18, a parent or guardian must sign. Terms, prices and conditions subject to change. Subscription subject to acceptance. Dorchester Publishing reserves the right to reject any order or cancel any subscription.

GET 4 FREE BOOKS!

You can have the best Westerns delivered to your door for less than what you'd pay in a bookstore or online. Sign up for one of our book clubs today, and we'll send you 4 FREE* BOOKS, worth $23.96, just for trying it out...with no obligation to buy, ever!

Authors include classic writers such as
LOUIS L'AMOUR, MAX BRAND, ZANE GREY
and more; plus new authors such as
**COTTON SMITH, JOHNNY D. BOGGS,
DAVID THOMPSON** and others.

As a book club member you also receive the following special benefits:
• **30% off all orders!**
• **Exclusive access to special discounts!**
• Convenient home delivery and 10 days to return any books you don't want to keep.

Visit **www.dorchesterpub.com**
or call
1-800-481-9191

There is no minimum number of books to buy, and you may cancel membership at any time.
*Please include $2.00 for shipping and handling.